永恆的莎士比亞改寫劇本 **9**

仲夏夜之夢

A MIDSUMMER NIGHT'S DREAM

William Shakespeare ◆ 著

Emily Hutchinson ◆ 改寫 ｜ 蘇瑞琴 ◆ 譯

MP3

永恆的莎士比亞改寫劇本 ❾

仲夏夜之夢

A MIDSUMMER NIGHT'S DREAM

作　　者	William Shakespeare, Emily Hutchinson
翻　　譯	蘇瑞琴
編　　輯	王婷葦
校　　對	高弘奇
內文排版	田慧盈
封面設計	林書玉
製程管理	洪巧玲
出 版 者	寂天文化事業股份有限公司
電　　話	+886-(0)2-2365-9739
傳　　真	+886-(0)2-2365-9835
網　　址	www.icosmos.com.tw
讀者服務	onlineservice@icosmos.com.tw
出版日期	2016 年 9 月 初版一刷

版權所有 請勿翻印
郵撥帳號 1998620-0 寂天文化事業股份有限公司
劃撥金額 600（含）元以上者，郵資免費。
訂購金額 600 元以下者，加收 65 元運費。
〔若有破損，請寄回更換，謝謝〕

國家圖書館出版品預行編目 (CIP) 資料

永恆的莎士比亞改寫劇本 : 仲夏夜之夢 /William
Shakespeare, Emily Hutchinson 作 ; 蘇瑞琴譯 .-- 初版 .--
[臺北市] : 寂天文化 , 2016.09
面；　公分
ISBN 978-986-318-497-3(平裝附光碟片)
873.43343　　　　　　　　　　　　　　105016491

Contents

Introduction

Long ago in Greece, Hermia and Lysander decide to elope. Demetrius, who loves Hermia, follows them into the woods, hoping to stop them. Helena, who is in love with Demetrius, also follows.

In the woods are a group of fairies and several craftsmen, rehearsing a play.

Puck, one of the fairies, tricks each character into falling in love with the first person he or she sees upon awakening. All sorts of humorous confusion follows.

Cast of Characters

THESEUS: Duke of Athens

HIPPOLYTA: Queen of the Amazons, a warrior race of women, defeated in battle by Theseus

EGEUS: An Athenian citizen

HERMIA: Egeus's daughter

LYSANDER: Young man who loves Hermia

DEMETRIUS: Young man who loves Hermia

HELENA: Hermia's friend who loves Demetrius

PETER QUINCE: A carpenter

NICK BOTTOM: A weaver

FRANCIS FLUTE: A bellows-mender

ROBIN STARVELING: A tailor

TOM SNOUT: A tinker (mender of pots and pans)

SNUG: A joiner (cabinet maker)

PUCK: (Robin Goodfellow) A fairy

OBERON: King of the fairies

TITANIA: Queen of the fairies

PEASEBLOSSOM, COBWEB, MOTH, and **MUSTARDSEED:** Four fairies who serve Titania

PHILOSTRATE: Theseus's servant

ACT 1

Summary

雅典公爵忒修斯與希波呂忒滿心期待兩人四天之後的婚禮。伊吉斯來找忒修斯說起他的女兒赫米婭，赫米婭拒絕嫁給狄密特律斯，反而傾心於她深愛的拉山德。伊吉斯請求忒修斯行使法律賦予他為人父親的權利——讓她選擇嫁給他所選的男人或是死亡；忒修斯同意了，赫米婭有四天的時間決定該何去何從。

拉山德與赫米婭決心結婚並離開雅典，他們計畫在午夜時分於森林相見；他們告訴了深愛著狄密特律斯的海麗娜這個計畫，而後者卻將之告訴了狄密特律斯，當狄密特律斯追隨赫米婭時她也尾隨在他身後。

於此同時，一群演員亦相約於森林中，綵排著將要在公爵婚禮上表演的戲劇。

Scene ❶ 🎧

(**Theseus** and **Hippolyta**, along with their **servants,**
enter Theseus's palace in Athens.)

THESEUS: Now, fair Hippolyta, our wedding
hour draws near. Four more days!
Time seems to go so slowly.

HIPPOLYTA: Four days will quickly become night.
Four nights will dream away the time.
And then the new moon, like a silver bow,
Shall look on our wedding night.

THESEUS: Go, Philostrate.
Stir up the youth of Athens to be merry.
Awaken the spirit of fun.
Tell all sadness to go to funerals.
We don't want any sad faces at our
wedding. *(Philostrate exits.)*
Hippolyta, I wooed you with my sword
In the heat of battle, and won your love
while defeating you.
But I will wed you in a different way—
With celebration, joy, and good times.

(**Egeus** and his daughter **Hermia** enter, along with
Lysander and **Demetrius**.)

EGEUS: Joy to Theseus, our respected Duke!

THESEUS: Thank you, good Egeus.
What's the news with you?

EGEUS: I am having trouble with my child,
My daughter Hermia.
This man, Demetrius, has my consent to
marry her.
But you, Lysander, have cast a spell on her!
(turning to Lysander) You have given her
poetry and exchanged tokens of love with
my child;
You have sung insincere songs of love by
her window in the moonlight.
You have given her rings, flowers, and candy.
You have used all the tricks young men use
On young girls like my daughter.
You have stolen my daughter's heart
And made her disobedient to me.
Now she refuses to marry Demetrius.
I claim my ancient right as a father:
As she is mine, I may give her to the man
I choose or send her to her death.
This is the law of our land, as you know.

ACT 1
SCENE 1

THESEUS: What do you say, Hermia?
    Let me remind you, fair maid,
    Your father should be as a god to you.
    He is the one who formed your beauty.
    To him, you are but as a form in wax
    That he has shaped. It is within his rights
    To leave the form as it is or destroy it.
    Demetrius is a good man.

HERMIA: So is Lysander.

THESEUS: In himself he is. But, in this case,
    Because of your father's wishes,
    The other must be seen as the better man.

HERMIA: I wish my father saw it with my eyes.

THESEUS: Rather, you must see it his way.

HERMIA: I beg your grace to pardon me.
    I do not know if it is proper for me
    To explain my thoughts to you.
    But I beg you to answer one question:
    What is the worst that could happen to me
    If I refuse to wed Demetrius?

THESEUS: Either to die or never to marry at all.
    Think hard, fair Hermia!

9

Consider your youth and your feelings.
Ask yourself if you could live as a nun.
Could you be a childless sister all your life,
Singing weak songs to the cold, lifeless moon?
Those who can do so are certainly blessed.
But would you be happy with such a life?

HERMIA: So will I live—or die—my lord,
Before I would marry a man I do not love.

THESEUS: Take time to think about this.
Tell us your answer in four days,

On the wedding day of my love and me.

By then you must prepare to die

For going against your father's will—

Or wed Demetrius, as your father wishes.

Or live as a nun for the rest of your life.

DEMETRIUS: Give in, sweet Hermia.

And you, too, Lysander.

Let me claim what is rightly mine.

LYSANDER: You have her father's love, Demetrius.

Let me have Hermia's. *You* marry him.

EGEUS: It is true—Demetrius has my love.

And so, I shall give him what is mine.

Hermia belongs to me. All my rights to her

I give to Demetrius.

LYSANDER: My lord, I am as good a man as he!

My family is as well-connected as his.

I have as much money as he.

My love is greater than his.

In every way, I am at least as good as he is,

And in some ways, I am better.

The beautiful Hermia loves me,

Which is the most important point.

Why shouldn't I return her love?
Demetrius courted Nedar's daughter,
  Helena, and won her soul.
She still loves this faithless man.

THESEUS: I have meant to talk to Demetrius
  about it.
But I've been so busy that I forgot to
  do so.
Come with me, Demetrius.
You, too, Egeus. I must talk to you
  privately.
As for you, fair Hermia, try
To fit your wishes to those of your father.
Otherwise the law of Athens will go
  against you.
We can do nothing about it—
You must die or vow to live a single life.
Come, my Hippolyta.
Demetrius and Egeus, you come, too.
I must talk to you about our wedding
And about something else that concerns you.

EGEUS: We are happy to go with you, my lord.

(**All** but Lysander and Hermia exit.)

LYSANDER: My love! Why is your face so pale?
How did your rosy cheeks fade so fast?

HERMIA: Perhaps it is from lack of rain.
Only my tears water them.

LYSANDER: Oh, my! From everything that I've
learned,
The course of true love never did run
smooth.

HERMIA: Oh, awful! To choose love by
another's eyes.

LYSANDER: War or death may stand in the way.
Love lasts just a moment, like a sound.
It is swift as a shadow, short as any dream
And as quick as lightning in a storm
That, in a rage, splits heaven and earth.
Before a person can say, "Look at that!"
The jaws of darkness eat it up.

13

HERMIA: If this is truly what love is,
It must be law. So we must be patient
And give to love our thoughts and dreams,
Our wishes and tears.

LYSANDER: Good advice, Hermia. Now, hear me.
I have a rich old aunt.
She's a widow with no children.
Her house is only 20 miles from Athens.
She thinks of me as her only son.
There, gentle Hermia, we can get married.

ACT 1
SCENE
1

Athenian law cannot touch us there.
If you love me, leave your father's house
Tomorrow night. Meet me in the woods,
Three miles outside of town.
Remember where I met you with Helena
To gather May flowers one morning?
That's where I will wait for you.

HERMIA: My good Lysander! I swear to you by
Cupid's strongest bow, and
By his best arrow, with the golden tip—
By all that keeps lovers' souls together—
And by all the vows that men have broken
(Which are more than women ever made)—
Tomorrow I truly will meet you there.

LYSANDER: Keep your promise, love.
Look, here comes Helena.

(**Helena** enters.)

HERMIA: Hello, fair Helena!

HELENA: You call me "fair"? You don't mean it.
Demetrius loves *your* fairness. You are
lucky! To him, your eyes are like stars.
Oh, were beauty as catching as sickness!

15

I would want to catch yours, fair Hermia.
If the world were mine, and Demetrius, too,
I'd give you the world and keep Demetrius.
Oh, teach me how to look like you, and how
To lead the dancing of Demetrius's heart!

HERMIA: He loves me though I frown upon
him!

HELENA: I wish your frowns would teach my
smiles such skill!

HERMIA: The more I reject him, the more he
loves me.

HELENA: The more I love him, the more he
rejects me.

HERMIA: He's a fool, Helena! It's not my fault.

HELENA: It's the fault of your beauty. I wish
that fault were mine!

HERMIA: Be happy. He won't see me again.
Lysander and I will soon leave this place.
Before I saw Lysander,
Athens seemed a paradise to me.
But I don't feel that way anymore.

LYSANDER: Helena, here's our plan:

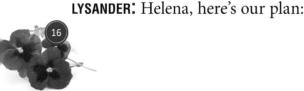

16

Tomorrow night, when the moon sees
Her silver face in the water,
We will steal away from A thens.

HERMIA: There we will meet new people and
seek new friends.
Goodbye, sweet childhood friend. Pray for us.
And good luck with your Demetrius!
Keep your word, Lysander, dear.
Meet me tomorrow at midnight.

LYSANDER: I will, my Hermia. *(Hermia exits.)*
Goodbye, Helena. As you love Demetrius,
may he also love you. *(Lysander exits.)*

HELENA: Some are so much happier than
others!
In Athens, I am thought as fair as she. But
what of that? Demetrius doesn't think so.
He does not see what everyone else does.
I love him just as he loves Hermia.
Love looks not with the eyes, but with
the mind.
That's why Cupid is always painted blind.
And that's why love is said to be a child—
Because its choices are often so wild.

Love often lies. Before Demetrius saw
  Hermia,

He swore that he was only mine.

(Suddenly Helena thinks of a way to see Demetrius again.)

I will go tell him of fair Hermia's plan.

He will follow her tomorrow night.

He might even thank me for the news.

If he does, I will not mind the pain,

For perhaps I can get his attention again.

(**Helena** exits.)

Scene ❷

(**Peter Quince, Snug, Bottom, Flute, Snout,** and **Starveling** enter Peter Quince's house in Athens.)

QUINCE: Are all the actors here?

BOTTOM: It would be best if you would call their names, man by man, following your list.

QUINCE: Here is the scroll of every man in Athens who is fit to act in our play. We will put on this play for the duke and duchess on their wedding night.

BOTTOM: First, good Peter Quince, say what the play is about. Then read the names of the actors. That way you get to the point.

QUINCE: All right. Our play is "The Most Sad Comedy and Most Cruel Death of Pyramus and Thisbe."

BOTTOM: A very good piece of work! Now, good Peter Quince, call your list of actors.

QUINCE: I call Nick Bottom, the weaver.

BOTTOM: Ready. Name my part, and go on.

19

QUINCE: You, Nick Bottom, are set down for Pyramus.

BOTTOM: Who is Pyramus—a lover or a hero?

QUINCE: A lover. He kills himself for love.

BOTTOM: That will cause some tears. If I do it, let the audience take care of their eyes. I will move storms! I will make them all feel sad! Yet I'd rather be a hero. I could play Hercules really well. That's a part I could really sink my teeth into! A hero is a great role. A lover is more to be pitied. Now name the rest of the players.

QUINCE: Francis Flute, the bellows-mender.

FLUTE: Here, Peter Quince.

QUINCE: Flute, you will play the role of Thisbe.

FLUTE: What is Thisbe? A wandering knight?

QUINCE: Thisbe is the lady that Pyramus loves.

FLUTE: No, I don't want to play a woman.
Look! I have a beard coming in.

QUINCE: No matter. You shall wear a mask,
and you may speak as small as you want.

BOTTOM: Let me play Thisbe, too. I'll speak in
a tiny little voice.
(speaking in a loud voice): "Thisbe! Thisbe!"
(then speaking in a small voice): "Oh, Pyramus,
my dear lover! I am your lady Thisbe!"

QUINCE: No, no, you must play Pyramus.
Flute, you will play Thisbe.

BOTTOM: Well, go on.

QUINCE: Robin Starveling, you must play
Thisbe's mother. Next, Tom Snout, the
tinker.

SNOUT: Here, Peter Quince.

QUINCE: You will play Pyramus's father. I will
play Thisbe's father. Snug, the joiner,
you will play the lion's part. I hope these
parts work out for all of us.

SNUG: Do you have a written copy of the lion's part? If you do, please give it to me now, for I learn slowly.

QUINCE: But it is nothing but roaring!

BOTTOM: Let *me* play the lion too! My roar will do any man's heart good. My roar will make the duke say, "Let him roar again. Let him roar again!"

QUINCE: But you would frighten the duchess and the ladies. They would scream. That would be reason enough to hang us all.

ALL: That would hang us, every mother's son.

BOTTOM: It's true, friends. If you should frighten the ladies, they would surely hang us! But I will roar as gently as any baby dove. I will roar like a nightingale.

QUINCE: You can play no part but Pyramus, for Pyramus is as sweet and proper a man as you would see on a summer day. That is why you must play this lovely gentleman.

(handing out the parts): Gentlemen, here

22

are your parts. I beg you to learn them
by tomorrow night. Meet me in the
woods three miles outside of town.
We will rehearse there. If we rehearse
in the city, we will be dogged with
company and our plan will be no secret.
I will draw up a list of props that we will
need for our play. Please, don't fail me!

BOTTOM: We will be there and rehearse
with great courage until we are perfect.
Goodbye.

QUINCE: We will meet at the duke's oak tree.
(**All** exit.)

ACT 2

Summary

精靈們於雅典近處的森林相見,彼此談論著精靈皇后提泰妮婭與精靈國王奧布朗的爭執。為了找提泰妮婭算帳,奧布朗要求喜愛惡作劇的精靈帕克,為他取來一朵珍奇之花,取此花的汁液塗抹在沉睡之人的眼皮上,會讓這人愛上醒來後第一眼所見的生靈。奧布朗計畫讓提泰妮婭愛上這座森林的某種生物,藉機笑話她。

狄密特律斯與海麗娜也來到此地,奧布朗偷聽了他們的談話。狄密特律斯告訴海麗娜他不愛她,告誡她切莫再跟上來;奧布朗聽完之後決心用這朵奇花的汁液來幫助海麗娜追求狄密特律斯的心。於是當帕克帶著花朵復返,奧布朗要求帕克將其汁液滴在「身著雅典服飾」的男人的眼皮上。

提泰妮婭在森林的另一隅陷入沉睡,奧布朗將汁液滴落在她雙眼上便離開了;赫米婭與拉山德也睡著了,帕克來到兩人身邊,並將汁液倒入拉山德眼中,隨即離去;狄密特律斯與海麗娜亦來到此處,狄密特律斯依然要求海麗娜莫要窮追不捨,就在狄密特律斯離開之時,海麗娜看到了沉睡中的拉山德,她喚醒了他,當拉山德一看到海麗娜,他馬上愛上了她並將赫米婭忘得一乾二淨。

Scene ❶ 🎧

(In a wood near Athens, a **fairy** enters at one door, and **Puck** enters at another.)

PUCK: Hello, spirit! Where do you wander?

FAIRY: Over hill, over dale,

    Through bush, through briar,

    Over field, over fence,

    Through flood, through fire,

    I do wander everywhere,

    Faster than the moon.

    And I serve the fairy queen.

    I place her drops of dew upon the grass.

    The tall flowers depend on her.

    In their gold coats, you see tiny spots.

    Those are rubies, fairy favors.

    In those freckles lie the flowers' aromas.

    I must go find some dewdrops here.

    And hang a pearl in every flower's ear.

    Goodbye, lively spirit! Our queen and all

      her elves will be here soon.

PUCK: The king gives a party here tonight.

    The queen must not come in his sight.

For Oberon is very angry. The queen has
   stolen a lovely boy from a king in India.
She wants him as her servant.
But jealous Oberon wants the child
To serve as a knight in the wild forests.
Yet she keeps the favored boy to herself.
She crowns him with flowers. He's her joy.
Now, every time the king and queen meet,
In wood or field, by clear water, or in
   starlight, they argue over the boy.
All their elves, out of fear,
Creep into acorn cups and hide there.

FAIRY: If I'm not wrong, I know you.
   Aren't you that clever, naughty sprite
   Called Robin Goodfellow? Aren't you he
   Who frightens the girls in the village?
   Don't you steal cream from milk,
   And play tricks on housewives?
   Do you not lead travelers the wrong way,
   Laughing when they get lost?
   You're the one they call "Sweet Puck"!

PUCK: You speak the truth.
   I am that merry wanderer of the night.

I joke with Oberon, and make him smile.

A wise old woman, telling a sad story,

Sometimes thinks I am a three-legged

   stool—until I slip out from under her,

And down she falls!

Then everyone laughs and laughs!

But look, fairy. Here comes Oberon.

FAIRY: And here is Titania, too! I wish that

   Oberon were gone!

(**Oberon** enters at one door, with his **attendants.**
Titania enters at another door, with hers.)

OBERON: I'm not happy to see you, proud

   Titania.

TITANIA: What, Oberon? Fairies, let's go.

   I don't want to see him, either.

OBERON: Wait! Am I not your husband?

TITANIA: Then I must be your wife. But I

   know how you sing songs of love to all

   the young girls.

Are you back from India so soon?

Have you come to see Hippolyta,

Your old love, be married to Theseus?

Did you come to wish them joy?

OBERON: How can you say that? For shame,
Titania, talking about my love for
  Hippolyta
When I know of *your* love for Theseus!
Didn't you lead him to break his promises
To so many women?

TITANIA: These are jealous lies!
Never, since the beginning of summer,
Have we been able to dance freely
On hills, in valleys, or in meadows.
You have disturbed our fun and our dances
By springs, brooks, and sandy beaches.
And so the winds whistle to no use.
In revenge, they suck up water from the sea
And flood the land. Rivers have grown so
  full they overrun their banks.
Farmers work and get no crops.
The green corn has rotted in the fields.
The sheep die in the muddy fields,
And crows grow fat on the dead flock.
The seasons are all mixed up.
The human mortals want their winter.
Snow falls in the fresh lap of the red rose,

And sweet summer flowers bloom in ice.

The amazed world does not know which
  is which!

And all this evil comes from our arguing.

We are their parents.

OBERON: Do you want to stop, then?

It's up to you.

Why should Titania cross her Oberon?

All I want is a stolen little boy

To be my page.

TITANIA: Set your heart at rest;

I would not sell him for all of Fairyland!

His mother was my friend.

And, in the spiced Indian air, by night,

We often talked as we sat side by side.

She sat with me on the beach's yellow sands,
  While we watched the tall ships.

We'd laugh at their sails, full and big-bellied

With the wind, as she was with that child.

Pretending to be a ship, she would

Sail upon the land and bring back gifts.

But alas! She, being a mere mortal,

Died when he was born.

It is for her sake that I raise the boy.
And for her sake I will not part with him.

OBERON: How long will you stay in this wood?

TITANIA: Until after Theseus's wedding day.
If you wish to see our moonlight fun,
And dance with us, come along!
If not, then stay away from me,
And I will stay away from you.

OBERON: Give me that boy and I will go
with you.

TITANIA: Not for your entire fairy kingdom!
Fairies, away!
We will keep on fighting if I stay.

(**Titania** exits with her **fairies.**)

OBERON: Go, then. You will not leave this
wood until I get even with you!
Come, Puck. Do you remember
That time I sat on a hill near the sea
And spied a mermaid on a dolphin's back?
She was singing such a sweet song
That the rude sea grew calm to hear it.

Certain stars shot madly from their orbits
To hear the mermaid's music.

PUCK: I remember.

OBERON: That same time I saw Cupid
Flying between moon and earth.
He took aim at a fair maiden below
And fired his love arrow at her heart.
But she moved out of the way, and
Cupid's arrow missed her.
I watched the arrow fall on a white flower,
Now made purple by love's wound.
Young girls call this flower "Love-in-
idleness."
Get that flower I once showed you.
The juice of it, laid on sleeping eyes,
Will make the soul fall madly in love
With the next live creature it sees.
Get it for me! Be back here again
Before a whale can swim three miles.

PUCK: I'll put a girdle around the earth
In 40 minutes.

(**Puck** exits.)

OBERON: Once I have this juice,
I'll watch Titania when she is asleep.
And drop it on her eyes. When she wakes,
She'll love the first thing she sees.
It might be a lion, a bear, a wolf, or a bull.
It might be a monkey or an ape. Whatever
it is, she shall chase it with love.
Before I take this spell away from her sight
I'll make her give the boy to me.
But who comes here?
Let me overhear what they say.

(**Demetrius** enters, with **Helena** following him.)

DEMETRIUS: I do not love you. Don't follow me.
Where are Lysander and fair Hermia?
You told me they were coming to this wood.
Go away, Helena! Follow me no more.

HELENA: You draw me like a magnet. My heart
Is true as steel. Lose your power to draw,
And I shall have no power to follow you.

DEMETRIUS: Draw you? Haven't I spoken fairly?
Haven't I told you the truth?
The fact is that I do not and cannot love you.

HELENA: And for that, I love you all the more.
   I am your dog, Demetrius. The more you
      beat me, the more I will follow.
   Treat me as you wish. Just let me,
   Unworthy as I am, follow you.

DEMETRIUS: It makes me sick to look at you.

HELENA: And I feel sick when I *don't* look at you!

DEMETRIUS: How can you chase after someone
   Who does not love you? Do you trust the
      night and this lonely place for safety?

HELENA: Your virtue will keep me safe.
   It is not night when I can see your face.
   So I think I am not in the night.
   And this wood does not seem lonely,
   For you, in my view, are all the world.
   Then how can it be said I am alone
   When all the world is here to look on me?

DEMETRIUS: I'll run and hide in the bushes
   And leave you to the mercy of wild beasts.

HELENA: The wildest has a kinder heart than you.
   Run if you wish. I'll change the story.
   The deer can catch the tiger

When cowardice chases and bravery runs.

DEMETRIUS: I won't listen anymore. Let me go.
Or, if you follow me, do not doubt that
I will do you harm in the wood.

HELENA: Yes, in the temple, the town, the field,
You do me harm! For shame, Demetrius!
Your wrongs offend all women.
We cannot fight for love, as men may do;
We were not made to woo.

(**Demetrius** exits.)

I'll follow you, and make a heaven of hell,
If I die by the hand I love so well.

(**Helena** exits.)

OBERON: Farewell, sweet girl.
Before Demetrius leaves this grove,
You will run, and he will seek your love.

(**Puck** enters again.)

Welcome, wanderer. Do you have the
flower?

PUCK: Yes, here it is.

OBERON: Please, give it to me.
I know a bank where the wild thyme blows,

34

Where every kind of lovely flower grows.

There Titania often sleeps at night,

Tired from dances and delight;

With the juice of this I'll streak her eyes,

And make her full of hateful fantasies.

(He gives Puck some of the flower.)

Take this and find in this grove

A sweet Athenian lady who is in love

With a man who hates her. Paint his eyes!

But do it when the next thing he sees

Will be the lady. You will know this man

By the Athenian clothes he wears.

Do this deed with care. Make sure he will

Love her more than she loves him.

Meet me here before the first rooster-crow.

PUCK: Fear not, my lord. Your servant shall obey.

(**They** exit.)

Scene ❷

(In another part of the wood, **Titania** enters, along with her **fairies**.)

TITANIA: Come now, a dance and a fairy song.

Then, for a while, go away from here.

(She points to different fairies.)

You will kill the worms that eat the roses.

You will war with bats for their wings

To make coats for my elves.

You will keep back the noisy owls that

Come here at night and hoot at us.

Sing me now to sleep.

Then do your jobs and let me rest.

(The fairies sing.)

FAIRIES: You snakes with double tongues,

Skunks and beetles, don't be seen.

Worms and lizards, do no wrong,

Don't come near our fairy Queen.

(**Titania** sleeps.)

A FAIRY: All is well. Now, away!

(**Fairies** exit.)

(**Oberon** enters. He places the flower juice on Titania's closed eyelids.)

OBERON: What you see when you awake,

As your true love you will take.

Love and suffer for his sake.

Be it pig, or cat, or bear,

In your eyes it will appear,

When you wake, as your own dear.

Wake when something vile is near.

(**Oberon** exits. **Hermia** and **Lysander** enter.)

LYSANDER: Fair love, you are weak

From wandering in the wood.

To tell the truth, I have lost our way.

We'll rest here, Hermia, if you think it good.

Let us wait here for the light of day.

HERMIA: Good, Lysander. Find yourself a bed.

Upon this bank I will rest my head.

LYSANDER: One spot can serve as pillow for us

both. Our hearts are as one.

HERMIA: No, Lysander. For my sake, my dear,

Lie farther off yet. Do not lie so near.

LYSANDER: Do not take me wrong, my sweet!

I mean that my soul is one with yours.
So let me make my bedroom by your side.
For lying that way, Hermia, I have not lied.

HERMIA: Lysander, you make a pretty riddle.
Now forgive my manners and my pride,
If Hermia meant to say Lysander lied!
But, gentle friend, lie farther off.
Such separation may well be said to be
    right for an unmarried man and a maid.
So stay at a distance—and good night,
    sweet friend.
May our love not change until life's end!

LYSANDER: And may my life end if I end love!
Here is my bed. May sleep give you rest!

HERMIA: With all my heart, may you be blessed!
(They sleep. **Puck** enters.)

PUCK: Through the forest I have gone
    But I have found no Athenian
    On whose eyes I might pour
    The loving juice of this flower.
(He comes upon Lysander and Hermia.)
    Night and silence! Who is here?

38

Clothes of Athens he does wear!

This is the man my master said

Hated the Athenian maid.

And here is the maiden, sleeping sound

On the damp and dirty ground.

Pretty soul! She should not lie

Near this man with no courtesy.

(He puts the flower juice on Lysander's eyes.)

Oaf! Upon your eyes I now throw

All the power this charm does know.

When you wake, let love keep

You so alert you cannot sleep.

So awake when I am gone.

I must now go to Oberon.

(**Puck** exits. **Demetrius** and **Helena** enter, running.)

HELENA: Stay—even if you kill me, sweet
    Demetrius.

DEMETRIUS: I tell you, go away! Do not chase
    me like this.

HELENA: Oh, would you leave me alone in the
    dark? Do not go.

DEMETRIUS: Stay at your own risk. I'm going
    on alone.

(**Demetrius** exits.)

HELENA: I am breathless from this chase.
    If I go on, I'm sure to lose face.
    Happy is Hermia, wherever she lies,
    For she has blessed and pretty eyes.
    Her eyes did not get bright with tears.
    If so, mine would be prettier than hers.
    No, no, I am as ugly as a bear,
    For beasts that meet me run away in fear;

So I don't wonder why Demetrius does
Like a monster, run from me thus.

(She sees Lysander sleeping.)

But who is here? Lysander, on the ground!
Dead, or asleep? I see no blood, no wound.
Lysander, if you live, good sir, awake.

LYSANDER *(waking and seeing Helena)*: And run
    through fire for you!
Dear Helena! Now I can see your heart!
Where is Demetrius? Oh, that vile word!
That name should perish on my sword!

HELENA: Do not say that, Lysander.
What does it matter that he loves your
    Hermia? Fair Hermia still loves you.
    So be happy.

LYSANDER: Happy with Hermia? I'm sorry now
For all the boring minutes I've spent with her.
I do not love Hermia! It is Helena I love.
Who would not trade a raven for a dove?
By reason is a man's heart swayed,
And reason says you are the worthier maid.
So far young reason has not been ripe.

But now I see that Hermia is not my type,
And reason leads me to your eyes. There I
   see love's stories in love's richest book.

HELENA: Why do you mock me like this?
What did I do to deserve such treatment?
Isn't it enough, young man, that I never can
Get a sweet look from Demetrius's eye?
Now I must hear you make sport of me?
Goodbye! I must say that, before this,
I thought you were a gentleman.
Oh, that a lady by one man refused,
Should then by another be so abused!

(**Helena** exits.)

LYSANDER *(to the sleeping Hermia)*: Stay, Hermia,
And never again come near Lysander!
It's as if I've eaten too many sweets.
My stomach is deeply sick of you.
I hate you. I turn all my might
To honor Helena, and be her knight!

(**Lysander** exits. Hermia wakes up.)

HERMIA *(alarmed)*: Help me, Lysander! Oh, get
   this crawling snake away from me!

Oh! I'm awake now! What a dream I had!

Lysander, look how I shake with fear.

I thought a serpent was eating my heart

   away—and you sat smiling as he did it.

Lysander! What, are you gone? Lysander!

Where are you? Say something, if you can

   hear. Speak! I'm almost fainting with

   fear.

No word? Then I know you are not near.

I'll either find you soon, or die right here!

(**Hermia** exits.)

ACT 3

Summary

當提泰妮婭在森林熟睡時,演員們來到此地。帕克用魔法將波頓的頸部以上變成了驢子頭,甦醒過來並看見波頓的提泰妮婭隨即愛上了他。

而奧布朗發現帕克將花的汁液滴錯了人,他非常憤怒,並決心要反錯為正;奧布朗將愛之汁液倒入狄密特律斯眼中,不久後,狄密特律斯一見到海麗娜便馬上墜入情網。海麗娜卻感到十分憤怒,她認為這兩個人都在嘲弄她。赫米婭與海麗娜爭執不休;奧布朗則責怪帕克造成這樣不堪的局面,前者計上心來欲導正所有錯誤。當這混亂的長夜終於將盡,四位愛侶紛紛在林中入睡(他們就在彼此身邊卻不自知),帕克將花液倒入拉山德的眼中。

Scene ❶ 🎧

(**Quince, Snug, Bottom, Flute, Snout,** and
Starveling enter the wood and see Titania lying asleep.)

BOTTOM: Are we all here?

QUINCE: Right on time. Here's a perfect place
for our rehearsal. This green area shall be
our stage. Those bushes will be
backstage. We will act out the play, just
as we will perform it before the duke.

BOTTOM: Peter Quince!

QUINCE: What do you say, Bottom?

BOTTOM: There are things in this comedy of
Pyramus and Thisbe that will never do.
First, Pyramus must draw a sword to kill
himself. The ladies won't want to see
such a thing! What do you say to that?

STARVELING: I believe we must leave the killing
out, when all is said and done.

BOTTOM: Not at all! I have a plan that will
make it all well. Write a prologue for me
to speak. Let the prologue say that we
will do no harm with our swords. Say

45

that Pyramus is not really killed. And just to make sure—say that I, Pyramus, am not Pyramus but Bottom the weaver. This will make everyone feel better.

QUINCE: Good! We will have such a prologue.

SNOUT: Won't the ladies be afraid of the lion?

STARVELING: I know that *I* will!

BOTTOM: You are right. To bring a lion in among ladies would be most dreadful! We should think about this.

SNOUT: We must say he that he's *not* a lion!

BOTTOM: No, you must say his name, and half his face must show through the lion's neck. He himself should say something like this: "Ladies," or "Fair ladies, I would wish you—" No, maybe it should be this: "I would ask you," or "I beg you not to fear! If you think I am a lion, you are wrong. No, I am no such thing. I am a man like any other." And then, let him say his name, and tell them plainly that he is Snug the joiner.

QUINCE: Very well, it shall be so. But there are still two problems. First, how will we bring moonlight in the room? As you know, Pyramus and Thisbe meet by moonlight.

SNOUT: Will the moon shine the night we are to present our play?

BOTTOM: Look at the calendar! Find out when the moon will be shining.

QUINCE *(taking out a calendar)*: Yes, it does shine that night.

BOTTOM: Why, then we may leave a window open in the room where we perform. The moon will shine in at the window.

QUINCE: Yes, and someone can come in dressed as the Man in the Moon. He could say he represents the moon. Then there is one more thing: We need a wall in the room. The story says that Pyramus and Thisbe talked through a hole in a wall.

SNOUT: You can never bring in a wall. What do you think, Bottom?

BOTTOM: One of us must play the wall. He can

have plaster or some mud on him, to
show he's a wall. Let him hold his fingers
open like this, and Pyramus and Thisbe
can whisper through that hole.

QUINCE: If that would work, then all is well.
Come, sit down, every mother's son, and
rehearse your parts. Pyramus, you begin.
When you have said your lines, go offstage.
Everyone else, do the same.

(**Puck** enters, invisible to those onstage.)

PUCK *(aside)*: What kind of clowns are here,
So near where the fairy queen is sleeping?
What—a play? I'll be the audience and
Perhaps an actor, too, if I see the need.

QUINCE: Speak, Pyramus. Thisbe, get ready.

BOTTOM *(as Pyramus)*: Thisbe, as sweet as the
flowers smell, so is your breath.
But listen! A voice! Stay here awhile
And soon I will appear to you.

(**Bottom** exits, into the bushes.)

PUCK *(aside)*: A stranger Pyramus has never
been played!

(**Puck** exits, following Bottom.)

FLUTE: Must I speak now?

QUINCE: Yes, you must. You must understand that he goes only to see about a noise he heard. He will soon return.

FLUTE *(as Thisbe)*: Pyramus, white as a red rose, Young, lovely, and as true as the truest horse, I'll meet you at Ninny's tomb.

QUINCE *(exploding)*: *"Ninus's"* tomb, man! And you don't say that line just yet. That's what you answer to Pyramus. Pyramus, you must enter. You missed your cue. Your cue is "truest horse."

(**Puck** enters with **Bottom**, who is wearing a donkey's head without being aware of it.)

BOTTOM: If I were fair, Thisbe, I would be yours alone.

QUINCE *(frightened by the donkey's head)*: Oh, a monster! We are haunted! Help!

(**Quince, Flute, Snout, Snug,** and **Starveling** exit, leaving only Bottom and Puck.)

PUCK: I'll follow you. We'll go in circles Through swamps, bushes, and woods.

Sometimes I'll be a horse, sometimes a dog,
A hog, a headless bear, sometimes a fire.
I'll neigh, bark, grunt, roar, and burn,
Like horse, dog, hog, bear, fire!
(**Puck** exits.)

BOTTOM: Why did they run away? This is a
trick they're pulling to make me afraid.
(**Snout** enters again.)

SNOUT: Oh, Bottom, you are changed. What
do I see on you? *(pointing to donkey's head)*

BOTTOM: What do you see? You see a donkey's
head like your own, don't you?
(**Snout** exits. **Quince** enters again.)

QUINCE: Bless you, Bottom! You are changed.
(**Quince** exits.)

BOTTOM: I see what they're up to. They are
trying to make a fool of me, to frighten
me, if they can. But I will not leave this
place, no matter what they do. I will
walk up and down here, and I will sing.
They shall see that I am not afraid.
(**Bottom** sings.)

"The blackbird, with its orange bill
The robin, with its song so true,
The wren with its little tail feathers—"

TITANIA *(waking up)*: What angel wakes me from
    my bed of flowers?

BOTTOM *(still singing)*:
    "The finch, the sparrow, and the lark,
    The gray bird with its song so plain—"

TITANIA: Sing again, gentle mortal. My ear is
    full of delight at the sound you make.
    My eye is delighted by your fine looks.
    Everything about you moves me
    To swear I love you at first sight!

BOTTOM: I think, lady, you have little reason
    for that. And yet, to tell the truth, reason
    and love are not good friends these days.
    It's a shame that people won't link them.
    That's just a little joke!

TITANIA: You are as wise as you are beautiful.

BOTTOM: I am neither! But if I were wise
    enough to get out of this wood, that
    would be good enough for me.

TITANIA: No! You shall stay here whether you
 want to or not.
 I am no common spirit.
 The summer is a servant to me.
 And I do love you. So, go with me!
 I'll give you fairies to bring you jewels
 from the sea.
 They will sing, while you sleep on flowers.
 And I will take away your mortal
 grossness, so you will be like a spirit
 made of air. Peaseblossom! Cobweb!
 Moth! Mustardseed!

(**Peaseblossom, Cobweb, Moth,** and **Mustardseed**
enter.)

PEASEBLOSSOM: I'm ready.

COBWEB: And I.

MOTH: And I.

MUSTARDSEED: And I.

ALL: Where shall we go?

TITANIA: Be kind and polite to this gentleman.
 Hop before him. Jump about in his view.
 Feed him with apricots and berries,

With purple grapes and green figs.
Give him honey from the honey bees.
And for candles, use wax from bees' legs
And light them with a glow-worm's eyes.
Show my love his way to bed and to arise.
Take the wings from painted butterflies,
To use as fans to wake his sleeping eyes.
Take care of him, fairies! Be considerate.

PEASEBLOSSOM: Hail, mortal!

COBWEB: Hail!

MOTH: Hail!

MUSTARDSEED: Hail!

BOTTOM: Greetings! What are your names?

COBWEB: Cobweb.

BOTTOM: I hope to get to know you better,
good Master Cobweb. If I cut my finger,
I will need you.
(to Peaseblossom): And your name, good sir?

PEASEBLOSSOM: Peaseblossom.

BOTTOM: Please, remember me to Mrs.
Squash, your mother, and to Mr. Peapod, your
father.

(to Mustardseed): And your name, sir?

MUSTARDSEED: Mustardseed.

BOTTOM: Good Master Mustardseed, I know you well. I've eaten many of your family with roast beef. I tell you, your relatives have made my eyes water! We must see more of each other.

TITANIA *(to the fairies)*: Come, wait on him. Lead him to my chambers. Tie up my love's tongue. Bring him silently.

(**All** exit.)

Scene ❷ 🎧

(**Oberon** enters another part of the wood.)

OBERON: I wonder if Titania is awake yet.

If so, I wonder what came to her eyes next,

That she now must love dearly?

(**Puck** enters.)

Here's my messenger. How now, mad spirit?

What mischief have you brought?

PUCK: Your wife is in love with a monster.

Near her chambers, while she was sleeping,

I saw a crew of workers—rude men

Who work for their bread in Athenian stalls.

They had met to rehearse a play to act

On Theseus's wedding day.

The most stupid and shallow one of them,

Acting the part of Pyramus, left the stage

And went into the bushes.

That is when I got my chance with him.

I set a donkey's head on his shoulders.

Soon his Thisbe called him. At this cue,

He left the bushes and went back to the

grassy stage. The other actors saw him

ACT 3
SCENE 2

With the donkey's head. Afraid of him,
They flew like wild geese from a hunter.
They rose and quacked and ran screaming.
  One fell and cried out, "Murder!"
Their sense was weak, their fears were strong.
They began to think that the bushes and
  thorns were grabbing at their clothes.
I led them on in their wild, confused fear
And left sweet Pyramus, changed, there.
Just at that moment, it came to be
That Titania woke, and loved a donkey.

OBERON: This is better than I expected!
But have you sprinkled the Athenian's eyes
With the love-juice, as I told you to?

PUCK: Yes, that's done, too. The Athenian woman was by his side. So, when he awoke, he must have seen her first.

(**Demetrius** and **Hermia** enter.)

OBERON: Hide yourself! Here comes the same Athenian.

PUCK: But it's not the same man!

DEMETRIUS: Why be so cruel to one who loves you so?
You should be so bitter with a bitter foe!

HERMIA: I've been patient until now, but I should treat you worse.
For you have given me reason to curse.
Have you killed Lysander in his sleep?
Have your shoes stood in his blood?
If so, your knife should kill me, too.
The sun was not so true as he to me.
Would he have left me sleeping in the wood?
I'd sooner believe that I could dig a hole
In the earth for the moon to shine through.
It must be that you have murdered him!
You look like a murderer—so dead, so grim.

DEMETRIUS: The victim would look dead,
And so should I.
I am cut to the heart with your cruelty!
Yet you, the murderer, look as bright
As Venus shining on a clear night.

HERMIA: What is this to Lysander? Where is he?
Oh, good Demetrius, give him to me.

DEMETRIUS: I'd rather give his body to my dogs.

HERMIA: Out, dog! You push me past the bounds
Of my patience. Have you killed him, then?
If so, you don't deserve to be called a man!
Oh, tell me the truth, for my own sake!
Did you kill him while he was sleeping?
Oh, you brave one! A snake could do as
much! Yes, a snake did it!
There was never a snake as bad as you!

DEMETRIUS: You are wasting your anger on me.
I did not kill Lysander.
He is not dead, as far as I know.

HERMIA: Then, please, tell me that he is well.

DEMETRIUS: If I could, what would I get for it?

HERMIA: This gift: never to see me again.

58

Now from your hated presence, I will go.

You won't see me whether he's dead or no.

(**Hermia** exits.)

DEMETRIUS: It's no use to follow her

When she's in such an angry mood.

I'll stay here for a while and rest.

(Demetrius lies down and goes to sleep.)

OBERON *(to Puck):* What have you done?

You have made a terrible mistake. You've

put love-juice on true love's eyes!

Now true love has turned false—

Not false love turned true!

PUCK: Then fate has taken over.

For every man who stays true to his love,

A million more break vow after vow.

OBERON: Go now, faster than the wind,

And Helena of Athens try to find.

Look for a woman who keeps making

Deep sighs of love, her heart all breaking.

Use some trick to bring her here.

I'll charm his eyes when she is near.

PUCK: I go, I go, look how I go,

Swifter than an arrow from a bow.

(**Puck** exits. Oberon puts the juice on Demetrius's eyes.)

OBERON: Flower, marked with purple dye,
When Cupid let his arrow fly,
Sink in the center of this man's eye.
When his true love happens by,
Let her sparkle in his eye,
Just like Venus in the sky.

(**Puck** enters again.)

PUCK: Captain of our fairy band,
Helena is here at hand.
And the man, mistook by me,
Begs her love, as you will see.
Lord, what fools these mortals be!

OBERON: Step aside. The noise they make
Will cause Demetrius to awake.

PUCK: Then the two will woo her at once.
That will be amusing to see.
I always think it's so much fun
To see humans come undone.

(Oberon and Puck step aside. **Lysander** and **Helena** enter.)

LYSANDER: Why would you think that I'm
making fun of you?
No one ever cries when he makes fun.
Look—I am weeping! Vows made in tears
Are vows that are true.

How can my feelings seem false to you?
I wear love's badge to prove them true.

HELENA: The more you say, the more you lie.
You said the same things to Hermia!
Will you leave her? Weigh your vows to her
And your vows to me on two scales.
They are the same—both as light as tales!

LYSANDER: I had no sense when I made
promises to her.

HELENA: And you have no sense now, by
breaking those promises.

LYSANDER: Demetrius loves Hermia, not you.

DEMETRIUS *(waking up and seeing Helena)***:** Helena,
my goddess! You are perfect, divine!
To what shall I compare your eyes?
Crystal is dull compared to them.
Your lips, like cherries, perfect to kiss!

When I see your hand, pure white snow
On high mountains seems black.
Oh, let me kiss your white hand now!

HELENA *(to both men)*: Oh, wickedness!
I see you both are making fun of me now.
If you were kind and had some manners,
You would not do this to me.
You must hate me to mock me this way.
If you were men, as you both seem to be,
You would not abuse a gentle lady
With your false promises and praise!
I know you both love Hermia.
What a manly game—to make fun of a
poor maid and make her cry!
No gentleman would act that way.

LYSANDER: You are not kind, Demetrius.
Don't be that way. You love Hermia.
You and I both know it. And here, with
all good will, with all my heart,
I give up my claim to her. She's yours.
So now give up your claim to Helena.
I love her and will love her until death!

HELENA: Never did fools waste more breath!

DEMETRIUS: Lysander, keep your Hermia.
If I ever loved her, all that love is gone.
My heart only stayed with her as a guest;
It has come home to Helena.

LYSANDER: Helena, it is not so.

DEMETRIUS: Don't talk about things you don't
know. Your words can put you in danger,
and you may have to pay for them.
Look who's coming—it is your love.

(**Hermia** enters.)

HERMIA: Dark night takes away the eye's power,
And makes it easier for ears to work.
As much as it hurts the sense of sight,
it doubles the sense of hearing.
I did not find you through my eyes.
My ears brought me to you, Lysander.
Why did you leave me that way?

LYSANDER: Why should I stay, when love for
another fair maid is pushing me to go?

HERMIA: What love could steal you from me?

LYSANDER: My love for fair Helena, who makes

the night brighter than all the stars.
Why are you looking for me?
Couldn't you see
That I left you because I despise you?

HERMIA: You do not mean this! It can't be true.

HELENA: Look, she is part of their plan!
Now I see that all three have joined
To make fun of me! Hurtful Hermia!
Most ungrateful friend! In spite of
    everything we two have shared, you treat
    me this way? We were like sisters!
We spent hours together!
We would feel sad that time was hurrying by
And parting us. Have you forgotten all
    our school-days' friendship? Hermia, we
    have embroidered one flower together on
    one sampler, sitting on one pillow.
We have sung one song, both in one key,
As if our hands, our sides, voices, and minds
Were one. We were like two lovely berries
Growing on one stem.
We were two bodies with one heart!
Now will you tear our old love apart,

To join men in scorning your poor friend?
It is not friendly—not how girls should be.
Other women would agree with me
Though I alone do feel the injury.

HERMIA: I am amazed at your passion. I don't
scorn you. It seems that you scorn me.

HELENA: Haven't you sent Lysander after me
To praise my eyes and face? Haven't you also
Sent your other love, Demetrius, to call
me goddess and heavenly? Why does he
Speak so to one he hates? And why does
Lysander say he does not love you?
Why does he declare his love for me,
unless you told him to?
I may not be as beautiful as you, or as
lucky—so hung upon with love. But a
person like me,
So miserable, loving but not loved—
Should be pitied rather than hated.

HERMIA: I do not understand what you mean.

HELENA: Yes, go on, with your fake sad looks.
Make faces at me when I turn my back,

Wink at each other. Keep the joke going.
It will be written down in history.
If you have any pity, grace, or manners,
You would not treat me like this.
Farewell. It's partly my own fault.
I'll end it by leaving.

LYSANDER: Stay, gentle Helena. Listen to me.
My love, my life, my soul, fair Helena!

HELENA *(bitterly):* Oh, that is excellent!

HERMIA: Sweet, do not scorn her so.

LYSANDER: Your threats are as weak as her prayers.
Helena, I love you. I swear it by my life.

DEMETRIUS: I say I love you more than he does.

LYSANDER: If you say so, prove it.

DEMETRIUS *(getting ready to fight):* I'd be glad to.

HERMIA *(taking hold of Lysander):* Lysander, what
is the point of all this?

LYSANDER: Get away, monkey! Let go of me,
Or I will shake you from me like a snake.

HERMIA: Why have you grown so rude?
Why have you changed so, sweet love?

LYSANDER: Sweet love? Get away, hated thing!

HERMIA: Are you joking?

HELENA: Yes, indeed, and so are you.

LYSANDER: Demetrius, my challenge stands.
I will keep my word with you.

DEMETRIUS: I wish I had it in writing.
I do not trust your word.

LYSANDER: What? Should I hurt her, strike her,
kill her dead?
Although I hate her, I'll not harm her so.

HERMIA: What? Can you hurt me any worse?

Hate me! Why? What is going on, my love?

Am I not Hermia? Are you not Lysander?

I am the same as I was yesterday.

Last night you loved me. Why did you go?

Oh, the gods forbid! Are you serious?

LYSANDER: Yes, by my life!

I do not wish to see you anymore.

So stop hoping, questioning, and doubting.

Be sure. There is nothing truer. It is no joke

That I do hate you and love Helena.

HERMIA: Oh, me!

(to Helena): You sneak! You thief of love!

Have you come by night

And stolen my love's heart from him?

HELENA: Fine, I see! Have you no shame?

Would you tear angry answers from my

gentle tongue? Shame, shame!

You fake, you puppet, you!

HERMIA: "Puppet?" So that is how the game

goes. Now I see how she has won him.

She has pointed out that she is taller than I.

And have you grown so tall in his view
Because I am so short? How short am I,
  you painted maypole? Speak!
How short am I? I am not so short
That my nails can't reach your eyes!

HELENA: Gentlemen, though you mock me,
  Do not let her hurt me. I have no gift for
    fighting. I am a lady, indeed. Don't let
    her hit me. Maybe you think, because
    she is something
Lower than myself, that I can match her.

HERMIA: "Lower?" Listen to her!

HELENA: Please, do not be so bitter with me.
  I have always loved you, Hermia, and I
    have never wronged you.
The only thing I did, loving Demetrius,
Was to tell him of your meeting in this
    wood.
He followed you. Out of love, I followed
    him. But he has told me to leave. And
    now, if you will let me go quietly,
I will return my foolish love to Athens
    and follow you no more.

Let me go. That's all I want now.

HERMIA: Why, go on! What's stopping you?

HELENA: The foolish heart I leave behind.

HERMIA: What? With Lysander?

HELENA: With Demetrius.

LYSANDER: Don't be afraid. She shall not harm you, Helena.

HELENA: Oh, when she is angry, she is strong!
She was a vixen when she was in school.
She may be little, but she is fierce.

HERMIA: "Little" again! Nothing but "low" and "little"!

(to the men): Why do you let her talk like that?

Let me at her!

LYSANDER *(holding Hermia back)*: Away, you dwarf, you mouse, you bead, you acorn!

DEMETRIUS *(to Lysander)*: You are too nice to Helena, and she does not want you. Leave her alone.

Don't take her side. If you show the smallest
Bit of love for her, you shall pay for it.

LYSANDER: Follow me, if you dare. We shall see
  Which one of us has more right to Helena.

DEMETRIUS: Follow! No, I'll go with you!

(**Lysander** and **Demetrius** exit, ready to fight.)

HERMIA *(to Helena):* This is all your fault.
  (Helena backs away.) No, don't go back.

HELENA: I do not trust you. I won't stay here.
  Your hands are quicker for a fight.
  My legs are longer, though, to run away.

(**Helena** exits.)

HERMIA: I am amazed. I don't know what to say.

(**Hermia** exits.)

OBERON *(to Puck):* Is this another mistake, or
    did you do it on purpose?

PUCK: Believe me, my king, I made a mistake.
  Didn't you tell me I would know the man
  By the Athenian clothes he wore?
  So how can I be blamed for putting the
    juice on an Athenian's eyes?
  And so far I am glad that it was done—
  For watching them fight is so much fun.

OBERON: Those men now seek a place to fight.
Go quickly, Puck, and make black the
night. Lead these rivals so astray
That they don't get in each other's way.
Talk to each in the other's voice.
Talk like Lysander, and stir Demetrius up.
Then talk like Demetrius, and stir up
Lysander. Lead them back and forth
until they fall in deathlike sleep.
Then put this juice in Lysander's eye.

(He gives Puck the flower.)

It has the power to undo errors.
Make his eyes see as they used to see.
When he wakes up, all this anger
Shall seem like a dream. The four lovers
Will go back to Athens. They'll always feel
connected by this night. While you are
doing this, I'll go see my queen
And beg her to give the Indian boy to me.
I'll break her love-spell for the donkey.

PUCK: My fairy lord, this must be done quickly,
For it is almost morning.
The ghosts that come out at night

Are now going home to churchyards,
Seeking their wormy beds. Fearing that
  day might look upon their shames,
They stay away from light
And only come out in the darkness of
  night.

OBERON: But we are spirits of another sort.
I have often danced in the morning light.
I've seen the sun rise over the sea.
But, still, you're right. Make no delay.
We may finish this business before day.

(**Oberon** exits.)

PUCK: Up and down
I will lead them up and down.

I am feared in field and town.
Goblin, lead them up and down.
Here comes one.

(**Lysander** enters.)

LYSANDER: Where are you, proud Demetrius?
Speak now.

PUCK *(speaking as Demetrius)*: Here, villain.
My sword is drawn. I am ready.
Where are you?

LYSANDER: I will be with you right away.

PUCK *(as Demetrius)*: Follow me, then,
To flatter ground.

(**Lysander** exits. **Demetrius** enters.)

DEMETRIUS: Lysander, speak again.
You coward, have you run away?
Do you hide your head in some bush?

PUCK *(in Lysander's voice)*: You coward, are you
Bragging to the stars,
Telling the bushes that you want to fight,
And not coming out? Come, you child,
I'll whip you with a rod. It would shame me
To draw a sword on you.

DEMETRIUS: Lysander, are you there?

PUCK *(in Lysander's voice)*: Follow my voice.
We won't fight here.

(**Puck** and **Demetrius** exit. **Lysander** enters again.)

LYSANDER: He runs and dares me on.
When I come where he calls, he is gone.
The villain is much faster than I.
I followed fast, but faster he did fly,
Now I am lost in a dark, uneven place.
I'll rest here. *(He lies down.)* Come, gentle
   day. Once you show me your gray light,
I'll find Demetrius, and we will fight.

(Lysander falls asleep. **Puck** and **Demetrius** enter again.)

PUCK *(in Lysander's voice)*: Ho, ho, ho!
Coward, why don't you come out?

DEMETRIUS: Face me, if you dare.
You keep running away. You don't have
   the courage to look me in the face.
Where are you now?

PUCK *(in Lysander's voice)*: Come over here.
Here I am.

DEMETRIUS: No, you are mocking me.
　　You shall pay for this,
　　If I ever see your face by daylight!
　　But for now, go your way.
　　I must lie down on this cold bed
　　And wait for the coming of day.
(Demetrius lies down and sleeps. **Helena** enters.)

HELENA: Oh, weary night! Oh, long, terrible
　　night! Cut short your hours! Rise, sun, so
　　I may go back to Athens by daylight,
　　away from these people who hate me.
　　Sleep, that sometimes shuts up sorrow's eye,
　　Take me awhile from my own company.
(Helena lies down and sleeps.)

PUCK: Only three? Come one more.
　　Two of both kinds makes up four.
　　Here she comes, hurt and sad.
　　Cupid is a wicked lad,
　　Thus to make poor females mad.
(**Hermia** enters.)

HERMIA: Never so tired, never so sad,
　　Damp from the dew, and torn by thorns,

I can go no farther. Here I will rest
Till the break of day.
Heaven protect Lysander if they fight!

(Hermia lies down and sleeps.)

PUCK: On the ground,
Sleep sound.
I'll apply
This to your eye.

(He puts the juice on Lysander's eyes.)

When you wake,
You will take
Great delight
In the sight
Of your true love's eyes.
And a saying that is well-known—
That every man should take his own—
In your waking shall be shown:
Jack shall have his Jill,
Nothing shall go ill.
The man shall have his mare again,
And all shall be well.

(**Puck** exits.)

ACT 4

Summary

提泰妮婭與波頓在她的寢宮中嬉戲歇
息,奧布朗與帕克則在兩人熟睡時前來。
奧布朗讓帕克施展魔法,除去波頓的驢子頭,並在提泰妮
婭甦醒前破除後者所中的法術。提泰妮婭醒了過來,她憎
惡波頓的模樣;她與奧布朗在四位雅典愛侶身邊翩翩起舞,
直到晨光來臨精靈們才離去。

忒修斯、希波呂忒與伊吉斯為了五朔節慶典進入森林,睡著
的四人紛紛醒過來並向忒修斯行禮,後者問起四人何以在
此——尤其拉山德與狄密特律斯本為不共戴天的敵人。拉
山德憶起前晚他本欲與赫米婭一同離開雅典;狄密特律斯
解釋他跟在這兩人後面,而海麗娜一路追隨著他,他說,不
知為何他對赫米婭的愛「如雪一般消融」,如今他只愛海麗
娜。

忒修斯命令這兩對愛侶應當成親,婚禮就在他與希波呂忒
的大婚典禮上一同舉行,這將會是個三喜臨門的婚禮!四
位雅典人仍分不清這是夢境抑或是現實。與此同時,波頓醒
來之後,記起了他無法解釋的奇妙夢境;他與他的演員夥
伴一起綵排接下來的表演。

Scene **1**

(In the wood, Lysander, Demetrius, Helena, and Hermia are lying on the ground, asleep. Enter **Titania** and **Bottom, Peaseblossom, Cobweb, Moth,** and **Mustardseed,** with other **fairies. Oberon** enters just behind, unseen by the others.)

TITANIA *(to Bottom)*: Come, sit on this flowery bed
>   While I touch your lovely face.
>   I'll stick roses in your sleek, smooth hair
>   And kiss your fair large ears, my gentle joy.

BOTTOM: Where's Peaseblossom?

PEASEBLOSSOM: Ready.

BOTTOM: Scratch my head, Peaseblossom.
>   Where's Mr. Cobweb?

COBWEB: Ready.

BOTTOM: Mr. Cobweb, get your bow and arrow
>   And kill me a red-hipped honeybee
>   On the top of a flower. Bring me the
>   honeybag.
>   Take care that it does not break or you'll be
>   covered with honey.
>   Where's Mr. Mustardseed?

MUSTARDSEED: Ready.

BOTTOM: Lend me your hand, Mr. Mustardseed.
And please, sir, stop bowing.

MUSTARDSEED: What would you like?

BOTTOM: Nothing, good sir, but a scratch.
I must get to the barber's, sir,
For I think I have too much hair on my face.
I am such a tender donkey.
If my hair tickles me, I must scratch.

TITANIA: Would you like some music, my love?

BOTTOM: I have a good ear for music.
Let us have the spoons and the bones.

TITANIA: And what would you like to eat?

BOTTOM: A bag of hay, or I could munch on oats.
I think I'd prefer hay. Good hay, sweet hay.
There's nothing like it.

TITANIA: I have an adventurous fairy who will get
nuts for you, from a squirrel's stash.

BOTTOM: I would rather have some dried peas.
But for now, let no fairies disturb me.
I am suddenly very sleepy.

TITANIA: Sleep, then. I will hold you in my arms.

Fairies, be gone.

(**Fairies** exit.)

Oh, how I love you!

(Bottom and Titania sleep. **Puck** enters.)

OBERON *(coming forward)*: Welcome, Puck!

Do you see this sweet sight?

I now begin to pity her foolish love.

A while ago, I met her in the wood,

Seeking sweet favors for this hateful fool.

I had an argument with her about it.

She'd put a crown of fresh and fragrant
  flowers on his hairy head.
Beads of dew stood
Within the pretty little flowers' eyes,
Like tears crying about their own disgrace.
When I told her what I thought,
She begged me mildly not to tease her so.
I then asked her about the child, which
  she gave me right away.
A fairy carried him to my chamber in
  Fairyland.
And now that I have the boy, I will undo
The magic that I placed on her eyes.
Now, gentle Puck, take this donkey's head
Off the head of this Athenian man.
Let him awake when the others do.
May all go back to Athens and think no
  more about this night's events.
Let them see it all as a dream.
But first I will set free the fairy queen.
(touching Titania's eyes): Be as you used to be.
See as you used to see.
This sweet bud shall have the power

To undo the magic of Cupid's flower.

Now, wake up, my sweet queen!

TITANIA: My Oberon! What a dream I had!

I thought I loved a donkey!

OBERON *(pointing to Bottom)*: There lies your love.

TITANIA: How did these things come to pass?

Oh, how I hate the sight of him now!

ACT 4
SCENE 1

OBERON: Silence awhile. Puck, take off his head.

(Puck removes the donkey's head from Bottom's shoulders.)

Titania, call for music. As for these five
    mortals, let them think they've been
    sleeping all night.

TITANIA: Let's have music to charm their sleep.

OBERON: Play, music. Come, my queen,

Hold my hand, and

Rock the ground on which these sleepers lie.

(Music plays. Oberon and Titania dance.)

Now you and I are like new friends.

Tomorrow at midnight we will dance in
    triumph at Duke Theseus's house.

We shall bless the house for the future.

And there, these two pairs of lovers,

Will happily be wedded.

PUCK: Fairy king, listen and hear:

A lark tells us that morning is near.

OBERON: Come, my queen, just like the moon,

Let's fly around the earth so soon.

TITANIA: Come, my husband, and in our flight,

Tell me what happened this night.

Why was I, sleeping, to be found,

With these mortals on the ground?

(**Oberon, Titania**, and **Puck** exit. A horn sounds.
Theseus, his **servants, Hippolyta**, and **Egeus** enter.)

THESEUS: Go, one of you! Find the man
 Who takes care of the forest and its
  animals.
 The May Day rite is finished,
 And it is still early enough to go hunting.
 Let my dogs loose in the western valley.
 Go, I say, and find the forest keeper.
(A **servant** exits.)

 (to Hippolyta): We will go, fair queen.
 On the mountaintop we will hear the
  music
 Of dogs and their echo joined together.

HIPPOLYTA: I was with Hercules once
 Hunting in the woods of Crete. They used
  dogs of Sparta to hunt for bear.
 Never have I heard such wonderful sounds!
 The trees, the skies, the fountains, and
  every place nearby
 Echoed together. I never heard
 So musical a sound! Such sweet thunder!

THESEUS: My dogs are that same kind, with
 Hanging jowls and sand-colored coats.

Their heads are hung with long ears that
Sweep away the morning dew.
And their voices are matched like bells,
Each tuned to each. A cry more musical
   was never cheered on with hunter's horn.
Judge when you hear.

(He sees the sleeping mortals.)

But, look! Who is this?

EGEUS: My lord, this is my daughter here asleep.
And these are Lysander and Demetrius.
This is Helena, old Nedar's daughter.
I wonder why they are here together.

THESEUS: No doubt they rose up early to watch
The May Day rite. They must have heard
That we planned to watch it
And came here to be with us.
But speak, Egeus. Isn't this the day
That Hermia must tell you of her choice?

EGEUS: It is, my lord.

THESEUS *(to a servant)*: Go, have the hunters
Wake them with their horns.

(A **servant** exits. A shout is heard from offstage. Horns
sound. The sleepers awake and kneel to Theseus.)

Good morning, friends. Valentine's is past.

Do these birds just start to pair off now?

LYSANDER: Pardon, my lord.

THESEUS: Please, all of you, stand up.

(They rise.)

(to Lysander and Demetrius): I know you two

  are rival enemies.

How, with your feelings of jealousy,

Can you sleep so close and fear no danger?

LYSANDER: My lord, I am still half-asleep.

I am amazed at this. Yet, I swear,

I cannot truly say how I came to be here.

For I believe—in fact, I know—that

I came here with Hermia. We planned

To leave Athens and go where we might

Be free from Athenian law—

EGEUS: My lord, you've heard enough!

I beg you, bring the law upon his head.

If they had run away, Demetrius,

They would have cheated you and me.

You of your wife, and me of my consent—

My consent that she should be your wife.

DEMETRIUS: My lord, Helena told me their plans.
    In anger I followed them. Helena followed
        me. Now I don't know what power—
    But some power it is—made my love for
        Hermia melt like the snow. Now it seems
    Like the memory of some toy
    I loved when I was a child.
    Today, my love, my heart, and my feelings
    Belong only to Helena. To her, my lord,
    I was engaged before I saw Hermia.
    But, like a sickness, I turned from her.
    Now, as in health, I have come back to her.
    Now I want her, love her, and long for her,
    And will be forever true to her.

THESEUS: Fair lovers, you are lucky we found
        you. We will hear more from you later.
    Egeus, I must rule against your will.
    For in the temple, by and by, with us
    These couples shall be wed.
    And, as the morning is flying by,
    Our hunting trip shall be set aside.
    Come with us to Athens, all of you.
    We'll stand together, three by three,

What a joyful wedding it will be!

Come, Hippolyta.

(**Theseus, Hippolyta, Egeus,** and **servants** exit.)

DEMETRIUS: These things seem like far-off
mountains that are only clouds.

HERMIA: I see these things with a sleepy eye,
And everything seems double.

HELENA: I think the same.
And I have found Demetrius, like a jewel,
Mine, and yet not mine.

DEMETRIUS: Are you sure
That we are awake? It seems to me
That we are still sleeping and dreaming.
Do you think the duke was just here,
And told us to follow him?

HERMIA: Yes, and my father.

HELENA: And Hippolyta.

LYSANDER: And he told us to follow them to
the temple.

DEMETRIUS: Why, then, let's follow him.
And along the way, let us tell our dreams.

(The **four lovers** exit.)

BOTTOM *(awakening)*: When my cue comes, call me, and I will answer. My next line is "Most fair Pyramus." Hello? Peter Quince? Flute, the bellows-mender? Snout, the tinker? Starveling? God's my life! They left me here asleep! I have had a most rare vision, a dream that even I can't explain! I thought I was—and I thought I had— Any man is a fool if he tries to say what I thought I had. The eye of man has not heard it. The ear of man has not seen it. Man's hand is not able to taste it. His tongue cannot think of it. His heart cannot feel what my dream was. I will get Peter Quince to write a ballad about this dream. It shall be called "Bottom's Dream" because it has no bottom. I will sing it for the duke toward the end of the play.

(**Bottom** exits.)

Scene ❷ 🎧10

(**Quince, Flute, Snout,** and **Starveling** enter Peter Quince's house in Athens.)

QUINCE: Have you sent anyone to Bottom's house? Is he home yet?

STARVELING: He hasn't been heard from. No doubt something has happened to him.

FLUTE: If he doesn't come, the play is ruined. It can't go on, can it?

QUINCE: It is not possible. No man in all of Athens is able to play Pyramus but Bottom.

FLUTE: I agree. He is simply the most talented working man in Athens.

QUINCE: Yes, and the best-looking, too. He has the sweetest voice!

(**Snug** enters.)

SNUG: Masters, the duke is coming. And there are more lords and ladies who were just married. If our play had gone on, we'd have made a fortune.

FLUTE: Oh, Bottom! He just lost sixpence a day for the rest of his life. He could not have escaped it. If the duke had not given him sixpence a day for playing Pyramus, I'll be hanged! He would have deserved it, too.

(**Bottom** enters.)

BOTTOM: Where are my friends?

QUINCE: Bottom! Oh, great day! Oh, most happy hour!

BOTTOM: Masters, I have wonders to tell you. But don't ask me about them! If I tell you, I am not a true Athenian. I will tell you everything, right as it fell out.

QUINCE: Let us hear, sweet Bottom.

BOTTOM: Not a word from me. All that I will say is that the duke is coming. Get your costumes together and tie up your beards! Meet at the palace. Every man look over his part. Let Thisbe wear clean clothes. And don't let the lion cut his nails, for they must hang out as the lion's

claws. And, most dear actors, eat no onions or garlic. This is a sweet comedy, and we must have sweet breath! No more words. Away, go, away!

(**All** exit.)

ACT 5

Summary

三喜臨門的婚禮結束了，希波呂忒與忒
修斯在宮殿內相談，當四位愛侶相偕而
來，兩人祝福他們在大婚之日喜悅與幸福。

波頓與演員們的話劇開始了，他們的演出毫無邏輯可言，然
而希波呂忒、忒修斯與其他觀眾仍然有禮的欣賞。當劇末之
時，忒修斯宣布美好夜晚的結束，並告訴兩對愛侶他們應於
兩週後的另外一個慶典再相聚。

帕克作最後的致詞，奧布朗、提泰妮婭與其他精靈為沉睡
的眾人施展魔法，他們翩翩起舞，並為熟睡的愛侶們祈福
祝禱。

Scene ❶ 🎧

(**Theseus, Hippolyta, Philostrate, lords,** and **servants** enter the palace of Theseus in Athens.)

HIPPOLYTA: My Theseus, it is a strange
Story that these lovers speak of.

THESEUS: More strange than true.
I don't believe in fairy tales.
Lovers and madmen have such seething
brains. They have more fantasies than
Cool reason ever understands.
The lunatic, the lover, and the poet
Have a lot in common.
The madman sees more devils than vast
hell can hold—the lover, just as crazy,
Sees Helen's beauty in the plainest face.
The poet's eye rolls from heaven to earth,
From earth to heaven. His imagination
Brings forth wonders and his pen gives them
shape with homes and names.
Strong imagination plays such tricks! If you
Imagine some joy, then there is imagined
Some bringer of that joy.

ACT 5
SCENE 1

Or in the night, imagining some fear,
How easily a bush can seem like a bear!

HIPPOLYTA: But all the stories they told
Are so alike! Their minds saw the same
fantasy. It seems like more than just
imagination.

(**Lysander, Demetrius, Hermia,** and **Helena** enter.)

THESEUS: Here come the lovers, full of joy and
happiness. Joy to you, gentle friends.
May joy and fresh days of love follow you
And remain in your hearts!

LYSANDER: More to you than to us!

THESEUS: Come, now. What plays and dances
Shall we have to while away these hours
Between our supper and bedtime?
Come, Philostrate, tell us!

(Philostrate comes forward.)

PHILOSTRATE: Yes, lord.

THESEUS: Say, what entertainment do you have
for this evening? What play?
What music? How shall we spend
This lazy time, if not with some delight?

PHILOSTRATE *(handing Theseus a paper)*: Here,
mighty Theseus, is a list of all who are
here this evening to bring you joy with
music or other entertainment. Choose
the one you like the best.

THESEUS *(reading from the list)*: "The battle with
the centaurs,
To be sung by an Athenian with a harp."
We'll have none of that.
"The riot of the drunken party-goers,
Attacking the singer in their rage."

That is an old play. I have already seen it.
"The three muses mourning for the death
Of learning." That is a sharp satire.
Not suitable for a wedding day.
"A tedious brief scene of young Pyramus
And his love Thisbe. A tragic comedy."
A tragic comedy? Tedious and brief?
That is like "hot ice." It doesn't make
   sense. What does this mean?

PHILOSTRATE: If this play had only ten words,
   It would be too long, my lord.
   The words are what makes it tedious, for
   In the whole play, there isn't one good word!
   My noble lord, it is tragic
   Because Pyramus kills himself in the play.
   When I saw it rehearsed, I must say,
   It made my eyes water. But my tears
   Came from loud laughter.

THESEUS: Who are the actors?

PHILOSTRATE: Hard-working men of Athens,
   Who never labored with thought until now.
   It's especially for your wedding day.

98

THESEUS: So we will hear it.

PHILOSTRATE: No, my noble lord,
It is not for you. I have seen it already,
And it is not worth seeing.

THESEUS: I will hear that play.
For nothing can be wrong if it is done
With simple good wishes. Go, bring them
in. And take your places, ladies.

(**Philostrate** exits.)

ACT 5
SCENE
1

HIPPOLYTA: I hate to see people embarrassed
By trying to do something they can't.

THESEUS: Why, gentle sweet, you shall see no
such thing!

HIPPOLYTA: But he says the play is terrible.

THESEUS: Let us be kind and thank the actors.
Good efforts by sincere people mean a lot
to me.

(**Philostrate** enters again.)

PHILOSTRATE: Your grace, the actors are ready.

THESEUS: Let them begin.

(Trumpets sound. **Quince, Bottom, Flute, Snout,
Snug,** and **Starveling** enter.)

QUINCE *(reciting the prologue)*: If we offend, it is
   with our good wishes.
   To show our simple skill is the true
      beginning of our end.
   We do not come, as wanting to please you,
   Our true intent is. All for your delight
   We are not here. That you should feel sorry
   The actors are here. By their show,
   You shall know all that you want to know.

THESEUS: This fellow does not make any sense.

LYSANDER: He says his lines like a rough colt.
   He doesn't know where to stop.
   A good lesson, my lord: It is not enough
      just to speak. You must try to speak true.

HIPPOLYTA: He talks like a child playing a flute.
   He makes noise, but it's all confused.

THESEUS: His speech was like a tangled
      chain—nothing broken, but all mixed
      up. Who is next?

QUINCE *(continuing the prologue)*: Gentle persons,
      perhaps you wonder about this show,
   But wonder on until truth makes all

things plain.

This man is Pyramus, if you must know.

Thisbe is the beautiful lady.

This man is the Wall, through which these
lovers whisper.

This man is Moonlight. You must know

By moonlight did these lovers meet

At Ninus's tomb, there to woo.

This is the Lion that scared Thisbe away.

As she ran, her coat fell to the ground.

The lion tore it with his bloody mouth.

Along came Pyramus, a sweet and tall youth.

He found his beloved Thisbe's bloody coat.

With a blade, he bravely stabbed his
burning breast.

And Thisbe, hiding in the shade nearby,

Drew his dagger out, and killed herself.

Let Lion, Moonlight, Wall, and lovers two

Tell the whole story through and through.

ACT 5
SCENE
1

THESEUS: I wonder if the Lion will speak.

DEMETRIUS: I wouldn't be surprised, my lord.
One lion may, if many donkeys do.

SNOUT *(as the Wall)*: In this play, I, Snout,
　Do play a Wall that has a hole. Through
　　this hole,
　The lovers, Pyramus and Thisbe,
　Did whisper often, and very secretly.
　This plaster and this stone do show
　That I am that Wall. The truth is so.

THESEUS: Could a real wall speak any better?

DEMETRIUS: It is the cleverest wall I have ever
　heard, my lord!

THESEUS: Pyramus is coming. Silence!

BOTTOM *(as Pyramus)*: Oh, blackest night!
　Oh, night, which always is when day is not!
　Oh, night! Oh, night! Alas, alas, alas!
　I fear that Thisbe has forgotten her promise.
　　And you, oh, sweet and lovely Wall,
　　That stands between her father's land
　　and mine,
　Show me a hole to look through.

(The Wall holds up his fingers.)

　Thanks, Wall. May the gods protect you!
　But what do I see? No Thisbe do I see.

Oh, curse you, wicked Wall, for lying to me!

THESEUS: The Wall should curse back.

BOTTOM: No, truly, sir, he should not.
"Lying to me" is Thisbe's cue.
She will enter now, And I will see her
  through the Wall. You'll see. It will
  happen as I told you. Here she comes.

FLUTE *(as Thisbe)*: Oh, Wall.
You have often heard me cry for
separating my fair Pyramus and me!
My lips have often kissed your stones.

BOTTOM *(as Pyramus)*: I see a voice! Now I will
  look through the Wall
To see if I can hear my Thisbe's face.
Thisbe!

FLUTE *(as Thisbe)*: My love!
You are my love, I think.

BOTTOM *(as Pyramus)*: Your true love I embrace.
I am faithful still.

FLUTE *(as Thisbe)*: And I, too, until the gods kill!

BOTTOM *(as Pyramus)*: Oh, kiss me through the
  hole in this vile Wall.

FLUTE *(as Thisbe)*: Alas! I kiss the Wall's hole, not your lips at all.

BOTTOM *(as Pyramus)*: Will you meet me at Ninny's tomb right away?

FLUTE *(as Thisbe)*: Alive or dead, I come without delay.
(**Bottom** and **Flute** exit.)

SNOUT *(as the Wall)*: I have played my part just so, And, being done, this Wall away does go.
(**Snout** exits.)

HIPPOLYTA: I never heard such silly stuff!

THESEUS: The best actors are only shadows. The worst are no worse, if imagination changes them.

HIPPOLYTA: It must be your imagination, then, and not theirs.

THESEUS: Let us imagine no worse of them Than they do of themselves. That will make them pass as excellent men. Look! Here come a man and a lion.

SNUG *(as Lion)*: Ladies, your hearts do fear The smallest mouse upon the floor.

You may now both shake and tremble

When a wild lion roars in rage.

Just know that I, Snug the joiner, am.

I'm not really a lion, just a man.

THESEUS: A most gentle and good animal.

DEMETRIUS: The very best beast I ever saw!

STARVELING *(as Moonlight):* This lantern is the

moon. And I am the Man in the Moon.

THESEUS: This is the biggest mistake of all.

The man should be put into the lantern.

How else can he be the Man in the Moon?

DEMETRIUS: He must be afraid of getting too close to the candle.

HIPPOLYTA: I am tired of this moon. I wish he would set!

THESEUS: He seems to be rather dim.

But, to be polite, we must stay and watch.

DEMETRIUS: Silence! Here comes Thisbe.

(**Flute** enters again.)

FLUTE *(as Thisbe)*: This is old Ninny's tomb.

Where is my love?

SNUG *(as Lion, roaring)*: Roar!

(**Flute,** as Thisbe, runs off, dropping her coat. Snug, as Lion, tears at it with his teeth.)

DEMETRIUS: Well roared, Lion!

THESEUS: Well run, Thisbe!

HIPPOLYTA: Well shone, Moon!

(**Bottom** enters. **Snug** exits.)

DEMETRIUS: Here comes Pyramus.

LYSANDER: That's why the Lion left.

BOTTOM *(as Pyramus)*: Sweet Moon, I thank you

For your sunny light.

I thank you, Moon, for shining bright.
I trust you to bring Thisbe to my sight.
But wait! Oh, no!
What dreadful sadness is here?
Eyes, do you see? How can it be?
Oh, sweet duck! Oh, dear!
You coat so good—
What? Stained with blood?
Come near, oh, terrible gods!
Cut the thread of my life! Crush me!
End me! Let me die!

THESEUS: This strong feeling,
And the death of a dear friend,
Would indeed make a man look sad.

HIPPOLYTA: Curse my heart, but I pity the man!

BOTTOM *(as Pyramus)*: Oh, Nature, why did you
make lions?
A vile lion has eaten my dear.
She is—no, no—she *was* the fairest lady
That ever loved and looked with cheer.
Come, tears! Destroy me!
Out, sword, and wound me!

Cut the left side of Pyramus
Where his heart does beat.
(He pretends to stab himself.)
So I die, like so, like so, like so.
Now I am dead. Now I have fled.
My soul is in the sky.
Tongue, lose your light!
Moon, make your flight.

(**Starveling,** as Moonlight, exits.)

Now die, die, die, die, die.

(Bottom, as Pyramus, pretends to die.)

HIPPOLYTA: Why does Moonlight leave before
Thisbe comes back and finds her lover?

(**Flute,** as Thisbe, enters again.)

THESEUS: She will find him by the stars.
Look! Here she comes.
Her speech ends the play.

HIPPOLYTA: I hope she will be brief. Such a
Pyramus doesn't deserve a long speech.

LYSANDER: She has seen him already
With those sweet eyes.

DEMETRIUS: And so she cries, as follows:

FLUTE *(as Thisbe)*: Asleep, my love?

What, dead, my dove?

Oh, Pyramus, arise!

Speak, speak! Quite dumb?

Dead, dead? A tomb

Must cover your sweet eyes.

These white lips, this cherry-red nose,

These yellow cheeks are gone, are gone!

Lovers, cry with me!

His eyes were green as leeks.

Oh, death, come to me

With hands as pale as milk.

Lay them in blood.

Tongue, not a word.

Come, happy sword;

Come, blade, soak my breast in blood.

(She pretends to stab herself.)

Now farewell, friends.

So Thisbe ends.

Goodbye, goodbye, goodbye!

(She pretends to die.)

THESEUS: Moonlight and Lion are left to bury the dead.

DEMETRIUS: Yes, and Wall, too.

(Bottom and Flute stand up.)

BOTTOM: No, I promise you. Their fathers have
  Torn down the wall that parted them.
  Would you like to see the epilogue?
  Or would you rather hear us dance?

THESEUS: No epilogue, please. Your play needs
    no explanation. Never explain.
  When the players are dead, none is to blame.
  If the writer had played Pyramus
  And hanged himself with Thisbe's stocking,
  It would have been a fine tragedy.
  And so it is, and very well-performed.
  But, come, let's see your dance.
  Forget the epilogue.

(The **players** dance, and exit.)

ACT 5
SCENE
1

  The iron tongue of midnight has rung 12.
  Lovers, to bed! It's almost fairy time.
  I fear we will sleep too late in the morning
  Because we have stayed up so late tonight.
  This play goes well with this night's slow
    pace. Sweet friends, to bed!
  Two weeks from now, once more let's meet.
  We'll celebrate with another feast.

(**All** exit. **Puck** enters, with a broom.)

111

PUCK: Now the hungry lion roars,
And the wolf howls at the moon.
Now the tired farmer snores,
With his weary work all done.
Now the firelight burns low.
Now the night owl, with its cry,
Reminds the man who lies in woe
That someday he will have to die.
Now it is the time of night
For the graves to open wide.
Each one lets out its sprite.
In the dark paths they will glide.
And we fairies now will run
By the moonlight's shining beam.
We flee the presence of the sun,
Following darkness like a dream.
Now we play. Not a mouse
Shall disturb this happy house.
I've been sent with broom before,
To sweep the dust behind the door.

(**Oberon** and **Titania** enter, with their **fairies.**)

OBERON *(to the fairies)*: Give glimmering light.
By the dead and sleepy fire

Every elf and fairy sprite

Hop as light as bird from briar.

Sing this song, after me,

Sing and dance—one, two, three!

TITANIA: Let the music gently float.

For each word, a musical note.

Hand in hand, with fairy grace,

We will sing and bless this place.

(Oberon leads the fairies in song and dance.)

OBERON: Now, until the break of day,
    Through this house we'll go our way.
    We'll visit every bride and groom
    And bless the air in every room.
    Bless the children they create,
    And make them always fortunate.
    So shall all the couples three
    Ever true in loving be.
    And ugly marks from Nature's hand
    Shall not in their children stand.
    With this magic fairy dew,
    Bless this palace, through and through.
    Through each room shall fairies race
    Bringing peace to this sweet place.
    And the owner of it, blessed,
    Always shall in safety rest.
    Dance away without delay.
    Meet me all by break of day.

(**All** but Puck exit.)

PUCK: If we players have offended,
    Think just this, and all is mended:
    That you have been sleeping here
    While these visions did appear.

And this weak and silly theme,

Means no more than just a dream.

Good people, do not hiss and boo.

Pardon! We'll make it up to you.

And, as I am an honest Puck,

If we have somehow had the luck

To escape your angry tongue,

We'll mend what's wrong before too long.

Or else the Puck a liar call.

So, goodnight unto you all.

Give me your hands, if we be friends,

And Puck will soon make amends.

(**Puck** exits.)

簡介

英文內文 P. 004

很久以前在希臘，赫米婭和拉山德決定私奔。深愛著赫米婭的狄密特律斯也跟著他們進了森林，希望能阻止他們；而愛著狄密特律斯的海麗娜也尾隨在後。

在森林裡有一群精靈，還有幾名正在綵排一場話劇的工匠。

其中一個精靈帕克，用計讓每個人醒來一睜開眼睛，就愛上他或她第一眼見到的人，於是出現了各種詼諧的混亂場面。

出場人物

P. 005

忒修斯：雅典公爵

希波呂忒：女戰士阿瑪宗族的女王，在戰鬥中被忒修斯擊敗

伊吉斯：一名雅典公民

赫米婭：伊吉斯的女兒

拉山德：深愛赫米婭的年輕人

狄密特律斯：深愛赫米婭的年輕人

海麗娜：赫米婭的朋友，深愛狄密特律斯

皮特昆斯：一名木匠

尼克波頓：一名織工

法蘭西斯弗魯特：一名修理風箱的工匠

羅賓斯塔佛林：一名裁縫師
湯姆斯諾特：一名補鍋匠（修補湯鍋和平底鍋的人）
斯納格：一名細工木匠（製作櫥櫃的人）
帕克（好人羅賓）：一個精靈
奧布朗：精靈王國的國王
提泰妮婭：精靈王國的皇后
豌豆花、蛛網、飛蛾與芥子：服侍提泰妮婭的四個精靈
菲勞斯特萊特：忒修斯的僕人

第一幕

●第一場———————————————————P. 007

（忒修斯與希波呂忒上，帶著他們的僕人們，走進忒修斯在雅典的宮殿。）

忒修斯：現在，美麗的希波呂忒，我們即將舉行婚禮了，再過四天！時間似乎過得好慢啊。

希波呂忒：四個白晝未幾即會化作黑夜，四個黑夜在夢境中打發了時間，然後新月將如同銀弓一般，高掛在夜空中俯視著我們的婚禮。

忒修斯：去吧，菲勞斯特萊特，鼓勵雅典的青年們歡欣慶賀，喚起歡樂的氛圍，讓所有的悲傷同赴葬禮吧，我們不希望在婚禮上看到任何傷心的面容。（菲勞斯特萊特下。）希波呂忒，我在戰鬥之中用我的劍向你求愛，在我擊敗你之時贏得你的芳心，但是我要用不同的方式來迎娶你——用慶祝、喜悅和美好時光。

（伊吉斯與他的女兒赫米婭上，拉山德與狄密特律斯亦隨之而上。）

伊吉斯：願忒修斯得到喜悅，我們尊敬的公爵！

忒修斯：謝謝你，好伊吉斯。你帶來什麼信息？

伊吉斯：我和小女赫米婭之間出了嫌隙。我將她許配給這位狄密特律斯，但是你，拉山德，對她施了魔咒！（**轉向拉山德**）你為她作詩，和小女交換愛的信物，於月光下在她的窗前唱著言不由衷的情歌。你送給她戒指、花朵和糖果，用盡年輕小伙子慣使以拐騙年少女孩的伎倆，就如同你拐騙小女這般。你偷走了小女的芳心，使得她不再順服於我。如今她拒絕委身於狄密特律斯，我要主張互古以來為人父親的權利：既然她是我的女兒，我即有權將她許配給我選擇的對象，或是將她處死；此乃我國律法的規定，你心知肚明。

忒修斯：你有何話要說，赫米婭？請容我提醒你，美麗的姑娘，你理應尊你的父親為天，他是給予你這般美貌之人；對他而言，你只是他塑造的蠟像罷了，他有權維持這個形貌或予以摧毀。狄密特律斯是個好對象。

赫米婭：拉山德亦然。

忒修斯：就他本身而言確實如此，但是在此例中，基於令尊的意願，另外那位才是較佳的人選。

赫米婭：但願我的父親能與我易地而處。

忒修斯：理應是你和他易地而處。

赫米婭：我懇求公爵閣下的寬恕。不知我予您解釋我的想法，是否合乎禮法，但是我懇求您回答一個問題：倘若我拒絕嫁給狄密特律斯，我可能面臨的最慘下場會是什麼？

忒修斯：若非被處死，就是終身不得嫁人。你要三思啊，美麗的赫米婭！想想你的青春和你的情感，問問你自己能否過著禁慾的生活，能否終其一生當個未有子女的修女，對著死氣沉沉的冰冷月光高唱薄弱的歌曲？那些做得到的人絕對是有福之人，但是要你這樣過完一生，你會快樂嗎？

赫米婭：所以在我同意嫁給一個我不愛的人之前，閣下，我就得這麼活著──或死去。

忒修斯：花點時間詳加考慮此事，四天後再給我們你的答覆；就在我的愛人和我的大喜之日。屆時你必須準備赴死，因你違背了你父親的意願──或是如你父親所願地嫁給狄密特律斯，抑或如修女一般度過你的餘生。

狄密特律斯：屈服吧，甜美的赫米婭；你也順服吧，拉山德，將理應屬於我之物歸還予我。

拉山德：你擁有她父親的愛，狄密特律斯，就讓我擁有赫米婭的愛吧；你儘管和他成婚。

伊吉斯：確實如此──狄密特律斯擁有我的愛，所以我要將屬於我之物送給他；赫米婭是屬於我的，我將我對她所有的權利轉交給狄密特律斯。

拉山德：閣下，我和他相較之下毫不遜色！我和他同樣出身於名門望族，擁有的財富也不亞於他，甚至我愛得比他更深。在各方面，我至少都與他不相伯仲；在某些方面，我是更勝於他。美麗的赫米婭愛我，這才是最重要的一點。何以不讓我回應她的愛？狄密特律斯曾與奈達的女兒海麗娜相戀，並把她迷得神魂顛倒；她仍愛著這個不忠誠的男人。

忒修斯：我本有意與狄密特律斯商談，但是我忙到忘了此事。隨我來，狄密特律斯。你也來，伊吉斯，我必須私下與你相談。至於你，美麗的赫米婭，盡量順服於你父親的意願吧，否則雅典的律法將對你不利，我們亦是愛莫能助——你必須死，或是宣誓終身不婚。來吧，我的希波呂忒。狄密特律斯和伊吉斯，你們也來，我必須與你們商談我們的婚禮事宜，以及其他和你們有關之事。

伊吉斯：我們很樂意隨你去，閣下。

（全體下，獨留拉山德與赫米婭。）

拉山德：我的愛人！你為何面容如此蒼白？你紅潤的雙頰何以褪色得如此之快？

赫米婭：或許是因缺乏雨水的滋潤，只有我的淚水在滋養它們。

拉山德：喔，天啊！據我所知，真愛的進程自古以來就不曾平順。

赫米婭：喔，好慘！竟要以他人的眼光選擇愛情。

拉山德：戰爭或死亡也許是愛情的阻礙。愛情如同聲音一般，只維持片刻；迅速如同浮光掠影，短暫有如夢境，彷彿暴風雨中的閃電似地迅雷不及掩耳，在狂暴之中開天闢地，在吾人說出「你瞧！」之前即被黑暗大口吞噬。

赫米婭：倘若愛的真諦非得如此，那就必定是律法，所以我們
　　　　要有耐心，對愛要多點思考和懷抱夢想，用願望和淚水等
　　　　候。

拉山德：說得好，赫米婭。現在，聽我說，我有個富有的老姑
　　　　媽，她寡居，膝下猶虛，住處距離雅典僅只二十哩；她視我
　　　　為親生的獨子。溫柔的赫米婭，我們可以在她那兒成婚，不
　　　　受雅典律法的約束。倘若你愛我，明晚就離開你父親的居
　　　　所，我們約在森林裡碰頭，就在城外三哩處。還記得某天早
　　　　晨，我與你和海麗娜相約一起採集五月花之處嗎？我就在
　　　　那兒等著你。

赫米婭：我的好拉山德！我以丘比特最堅韌的弓對你起誓，以
　　　　他最好的、黃金製箭尖的箭，──以守護情人們靈魂永不
　　　　分離的一切──也以男人們打破的所有盟約（比女人們曾
　　　　立下的誓言更多）向你起誓──明天我們不見不散。

拉山德：你務必信守承諾，愛人。瞧，海麗娜來了。

（海麗娜上。）

赫米婭：嗨，美麗的海麗娜！

海麗娜：你稱我為「美麗」？你這是玩笑話，狄密特律斯愛的
　　　　就是你的美麗。你可真幸運！對他而言，你的雙眼有如星
　　　　辰。喔，但願美麗如同疾病似地會傳染！我倒是想感染你
　　　　的美貌，美麗的赫米婭。倘若全世界皆為我所有，狄密特律
　　　　斯亦然，我寧願給你全世界，獨留狄密特律斯。喔，教我如
　　　　何擁有你這般的美貌，如何占滿狄密特律斯的心！

赫米婭：縱使我對他蹙眉，他仍然愛我！

海麗娜：但願我的笑容能有你的蹙眉那般的魔力！

赫米婭：我愈是拒絕他，他就愈是愛我。

海麗娜：我愈是愛他，他就愈是拒我於千里之外。

赫米婭：他是個傻瓜，海麗娜！這並非我的錯。

海麗娜：錯的是你的美貌，但願犯下那個錯的是我！

赫米婭：開心一點，他不會再見到我了，我和拉山德未幾即將離開此地。在我見到拉山德之前，雅典於我似乎是個仙境，但是此刻我已完全改觀。

拉山德：海麗娜，我們的計畫是這樣的：明晚在月升倒映水面之時，我們會悄然離開雅典。

赫米婭：我們會去那裡認識新的人、結交新的朋友。再見了，甜美的兒時好友，為我們禱告吧，也祝福你和你的狄密特律斯！你要言而有信，親愛的拉山德，明晚午夜不見不散。

拉山德：我會準時赴約，我的赫米婭。（赫米婭下。）再見了，海麗娜。你深愛著狄密特律斯，但願他也能愛你。（拉山德下。）

海麗娜：有些人就是比別人更快樂許多！在雅典，我的美貌與她難分軒輊，但是那又如何？狄密特律斯並不這麼認為，他的眼光不同於他人。我愛他一如他愛赫米婭；愛情不是以眼看人，而是以心看人，所以畫中的丘比特永遠是眼盲的，也因此愛情被比擬為一個小孩──因它的選擇經常是如此瘋狂。愛情屢屢說謊；在狄密特律斯見到赫米婭之前，他發誓他只屬於我一人。（海麗娜突然想到一個再見到狄密特律斯的方法。）我要去將美麗的赫米婭的計畫告知予他，他明晚必會跟蹤她，或許他甚至會感謝我通報他此事。倘若他感謝我，我不會在意心中的苦痛，因為我或許能再得到他的關注。

（海麗娜下。）

●第二場 ─────────────────────── P. 019

（皮特昆斯、斯納格、波頓、弗魯特、斯諾特與斯塔佛林上，走進皮特
　昆斯位於雅典的住家。）

昆斯：所有演員們都到齊了嗎？

波頓：你最好還是點個名，照著你的名單逐一確認。

昆斯：這個卷軸記載了適合演出我們話劇的每一個雅典人，我
　　　　們要在公爵與公爵夫人的婚禮當晚演出這場話劇。

波頓：首先，好皮特昆斯，說說這場話劇的情節，接著念出演
　　　　員們的姓名，如此便能摘要出重點。

昆斯：好的，我們的話劇名為「皮拉姆斯與提絲比最悲傷的喜
　　　　劇和最悲慘的死亡」。

波頓：非常好的一部傑作！現在，好皮特昆斯，念出演員名單
　　　　吧。

昆斯：我點名織工尼克波頓。

波頓：在此。念出我的角色，然後繼續。

昆斯：你，尼克波頓，扮演的是皮拉姆斯。

波頓：皮拉姆斯是何人──是情種或是英雄？

昆斯：是情種，他為愛而自盡殉情。

波頓：那會引人熱淚。若要我扮演此角，就讓觀眾們好好保重
　　　　他們的眼睛；暴風雨亦會為我所感動！我會使他們同感悲
　　　　傷！但是我寧可扮演英雄，海克力士一角我能演得很好；
　　　　這是我真的能完全融入的角色！英雄是偉大的角色，情種
　　　　是被同情的成份居多。現在繼續點名其他的演員吧。

昆斯：修風箱工匠法蘭西斯弗魯特。

弗魯特：在此，皮特昆斯。

昆斯：弗魯特，你要扮演的角色是提絲比。

弗魯特：提絲比是何人？流浪的騎士？

昆斯：提絲比是皮拉姆斯深愛的女士。

弗魯特：不，我不想演個女人。瞧！我還生出鬍子了。

昆斯：無妨，你就戴上面具吧，說話的聲音盡量細一點。

波頓：讓我也來扮演提絲比，我會用細細的聲音說話。（大聲說：）「提絲比！提絲比！」（然後小聲說：）「喔，皮拉姆斯，我親愛的愛人！我是你心愛的女士提絲比！」

昆斯：不、不，你必須扮演皮拉姆斯。弗魯特，你來扮演提絲比。

波頓：繼續念吧。

昆斯：羅賓斯塔佛林，你來扮演提絲比的母親。接下來是補鍋匠斯諾特。

斯諾特：在此，皮特昆斯。

昆斯：你來扮演皮拉姆斯的父親，提絲比的父親由我扮演。細工木匠斯納格，你扮演獅子的角色。希望我們都能勝任各自的角色。

斯納格：你有寫下獅子一角的台詞嗎？倘若你有，請現在就交給我，因我學得很慢。

昆斯：但是獅子就只有吼叫啊！

波頓：讓我也來扮演獅子吧！我的吼叫聲能取悅任何人。我的吼叫聲會使公爵大喊：「讓他再吼一聲，讓他再吼一聲！」

昆斯：但是你會嚇壞公爵夫人和在場的女士們，她們會驚聲
　　　尖叫，為此就足夠讓我們都被絞死了。

全體：會害我們被絞死，每個母親所生的兒子。

波頓：這倒是真的，朋友們。倘若你們嚇壞了女士們，他們必
　　　定會絞死我們！但是我會盡量輕聲吼叫，像隻乳鴿一般；
　　　我會像夜鶯似地吼叫。

昆斯：你就只能扮演皮拉姆斯一角，因皮拉姆斯是你在夏日
　　　會見到的溫恭又彬彬有禮的男士，所以你必須扮演這位可
　　　親的紳士。（**分配劇本**：）先生們，這是你們的劇本，請你們
　　　在明晚以前熟記於心。到城外三哩處的森林裡找我，我們
　　　就在那兒綵排。倘若我們在市區綵排，必定有人會亦步亦
　　　趨，我們的計畫就無法保密了。我會擬出一份我們話劇需
　　　要的道具清單，請各位莫要令我失望！

波頓：我們會準時赴約，鼓起勇氣綵排，直到我們演得完美為
　　　止。再見。

昆斯：我們就相約在公爵的橡樹底下。

（全體下。）

第二幕

● 第一場 ────────────────── P. 025

（在雅典附近的一座森林裡，一個精靈從一扇門上，帕克從另一扇門
上。）

帕克：嗨，精靈！你在何處遊蕩？

精靈：在山頭、在山谷，穿過樹林、荊棘叢，越過原野、圍籬，
穿越洪水、大火，我無處不遊蕩，速度比月亮更快。我還得
服侍精靈皇后，我將她的露珠置於青草之上，高大的花朵
皆要倚賴她。你在他們的金色外衣上看到的小亮點，都是
精靈贈與的紅寶石，那些小斑點有著百花的芳香。我得去
找點露珠了，在每朵花的耳上掛一顆珍珠。再見，活潑的精
靈！我們皇后和她所有的小精靈們，未幾即會來到此地。

帕克：國王今晚將在此舉辦宴會，皇后必不能出現在他的眼
前，因為奧布朗非常生氣。皇后偷了印度一位國王的可愛小
男孩，作為她的僕人之用，但是善妒的奧布朗也想要這個
孩子，在荒野的森林裡擔任騎士。然而，她獨占了這個得天
獨厚的男孩，用花環給他加冠；他令她滿心喜悅。如今，每
當國王和皇后見面，不論在森林或原野、清澈的水邊或星
空之下，他們都會為這男孩而爭吵。他們所有的小精靈們，
都會嚇得躲進橡實殼裡藏起來。

精靈：倘若我沒認錯人，我認識你，你不就是那個聰明又淘
氣、名喚好人羅賓的精靈嗎？在村子裡嚇壞女孩們的不就
是你？你不是偷走牛奶的乳脂，還對主婦們惡作劇？你不
是故意領旅人們走錯路，在他們迷路時還嘲笑他們？你就
是人稱的「好帕克」！

帕克：你的話句句屬實，我是夜裡快活的遊蕩者，我對著奧布朗惡作劇，逗他發笑。有個睿智的老婦人在敘述一個悲傷的故事，她有時會把我當成三隻腳的椅凳——直到我從她底下偷溜出來，害她摔得四腳朝天！然後每個人都捧腹大笑！但是你瞧，精靈，奧布朗來了。

精靈：提泰妮婭也來了！但願奧布朗能快快離開！

（奧布朗從一扇門上，帶著他的侍從們。提泰妮婭從另一扇門上，帶著她的侍從們。）

奧布朗：我並不開心見到你，驕傲的提泰妮婭。

提泰妮婭：怎麼，奧布朗？精靈們，我們走，我也不想見到他。

奧布朗：等等！我不是你的夫君嗎？

提泰妮婭：那我必定是你的妻子，但是我知道你四處唱情歌給年輕女孩聽。你這麼快就從印度回來了？你是來看著你的舊愛希波呂忒嫁給忒修斯嗎？你是來祝福他們嗎？

奧布朗：你怎能口出此言？真可恥，提泰妮婭，你還說希波呂忒是我的舊愛，你對忒修斯的愛我也是心知肚明！你不是引導他違背了他對眾多女子的承諾嗎？

提泰妮婭：這些都是你出於嫉妒的謊言！自從初夏以來，我們從未得以在山頭、山谷或草原上恣意起舞。你破壞了我們的興致，打擾我們在泉畔、溪邊和沙灘上跳舞，於是風再颼颼作響也無用，而他們為了報復，吸光了海水淹沒整個陸地，河川的水位高漲潰堤，農民們辛苦勞動卻收成不了作物。綠色的玉米在田裡腐爛，綿羊死在泥濘的原野上，烏鴉們卻因飽食牲畜的屍體而日益肥胖。四季全都大亂，凡人祈求冬天再返。白雪飄降在紅玫瑰初綻的膝上，夏天美麗的花朵卻在冰雪中盛開，世人已驚愕得不知萬物秩序！這邪惡的一切皆因我們的爭執而起，我們是萬物的父母啊。

奧布朗：那你想到此為止嗎？由你決定。提泰妮婭何以要惹惱她的奧布朗？我只想要她偷來的小男孩當我的童僕啊。

提泰妮婭：你死了這條心吧，即使用整個精靈王國來交換，我也不同意！他的母親生前是我的好友，我們經常在瀰漫香料氣味的印度夜晚，並肩坐著聊天。她陪我坐在海邊的黃沙上，我們一起看著高大的船隻，嘲笑它們的船帆被風吹得鼓脹，如同她身懷六甲隆起的肚子一般。她假裝自己是一艘船，在陸地上航行，帶著禮物回來。但是，哎呀！她只不過是個凡人，在產下他之後便香消玉殞。男孩交給我撫養是為了她好；為了她，我萬萬不能與他分開。

奧布朗：你會在這森林裡待多久？

提泰妮婭：等到忒修斯的婚禮過後。倘若你想看我們在月光下尋歡作樂，與我們共舞，那你就來吧！倘若你不想，那就離我遠一點，我也會離你遠遠的。

奧布朗：把那男孩給我，我就隨你去。

提泰妮婭：即使你用整個精靈王國來交換，我也辦不到！精靈們，走吧！倘若我久留此地，我們必會爭吵不休。

（*提泰妮婭帶著她的精靈們下。*）

奧布朗：去吧，在我和你扯平之前，不准你離開這座森林！來，帕克，你是否記得有次我坐在海邊的山頭上，看到海豚背上有美人魚？她當時正唱著悠美的歌曲，洶湧的海浪一聽到就平靜了下來；有些星星聽到美人魚的歌聲，還瘋狂地偏離了軌道。

帕克：我記得。

奧布朗：那次我看到丘比特在月亮和陸地之間飛舞，他瞄準了地面上的一個美麗的少女，要用他的愛之箭射向她的心

坎。但是她突然移開，丘比特的箭並未射中她。我看著那支箭落在一朵白花上，使之因愛的傷口而變成紫色。年輕女孩稱這種花為「徒勞的愛（編注：三色菫）」；我曾給你看過那種花，去取來給我，將其汁液塗抹在沉睡的眼皮上，就能使靈魂瘋狂愛上睜眼後初見的生物。去取來給我！在鯨魚悠游三哩之前趕回此地。

帕克：四十分鐘以內，我即可為地球圍上腰帶。

（帕克下。）

奧布朗：一旦我取得此花的汁液，我會在提泰妮婭沉睡時看著她，將之滴在她的眼皮上，待她醒來之後就會愛上她見到的第一樣東西，可能是獅子、熊、狼或公牛，又或許是猴子或猩猩；不論是什麼，她將懷著愛意窮追不捨。在我消除她身受的魔咒之前，我會命她將那男孩交予我。但是來者何人？讓我來偷聽他們的談話。

（狄密特律斯上，海麗娜緊追於後。）

狄密特律斯：我並不愛你，莫要尾隨我。拉山德和美麗的赫米婭在哪兒？你說他們要來這座森林。你走吧，海麗娜！莫要再跟著我了。

海麗娜：你有如磁鐵一般吸引著我，我的心有如鋼鐵似地真誠。一旦你失去吸引力，我便無力再跟隨你。

狄密特律斯：吸引著你？我說得不夠明確嗎？難道我未曾對你表明事實？其實我根本不愛你，也不可能愛你。

海麗娜：為此我就更愛你了。我是你的狗，狄密特律斯，你愈是毆打我，我就愈要跟著你。任憑你隨意待我，只消讓卑微的我跟著你便是。

狄密特律斯：看著你令我作嘔。

海麗娜：而我不看著你就會生病。

狄密特律斯：你怎能對一個不愛你的人窮追不捨？你相信夜晚和這個偏僻之處能保你平安嗎？

海麗娜：你的美德將保我平安。我能看清你的臉就不是夜晚，所以我想我並不身處黑夜，而這座森林亦未看似偏僻，因為你在我眼前就是全世界。全世界都在我眼前看著我，又何以說我是孤身一人？

狄密特律斯：我將奔向樹叢中躲藏，任憑你被野獸處置。

海麗娜：最狂野的野獸亦比你更有良心。你儘管跑吧，我來修改故事的情節：鹿可以捕捉老虎，懦弱的要追獵、而勇敢的要逃竄。

狄密特律斯：我不想再聽下去了。讓我走，否則倘若你再跟著我，莫要懷疑我會在這森林裡對你不利。

海麗娜：好啊，在神殿、城鎮、原野，你大可對我不利！可惜啊，狄密特律斯！你犯的錯觸怒了所有的女人。我們無法如同男人可能會做的一般為愛而戰；我們並非生來求愛的。（狄密特律斯下。）我會跟隨你，倘若我死在我深愛的人手裡，那地獄就將化為天堂。

（海麗娜下。）

奧布朗：再會了，甜美的女孩。在狄密特律斯離開這座小樹林之前，你會奔跑，他會苦追你的愛情。（帕克再上。）歡迎你，流浪的人，你可取到那花了？

帕克：是的，就在這兒。

奧布朗：請你交予我。我知道有個開滿野生百里香的河堤，那兒生長著各種不同的美麗花朵；每晚提泰妮婭在歌舞狂歡至疲累之後，經常在那兒入睡，我要用這花的汁液塗在她的眼皮上，使她充滿可憎的幻想。（他將一些花交予帕克。）這個給你，在這小樹林裡找到一位甜美的雅典女子，她深愛著一個憎惡她的男人。將這汁液塗在他的眼皮上！但是你要確定他睜開眼第一個看到的，會是那名女子；此人身穿雅典服飾，你一看便知。此事你要審慎行之，確定他會愛她更甚於她愛他。在第一聲雞啼之前，在此處與我碰頭。

帕克： 莫要擔心，陛下，你的僕人必不辱使命。

（他們下。）

●第二場 ———————————————P. 036

（在森林裡的另一處。提泰妮婭上，她的精靈們隨侍在側。）

提泰妮婭： 來吧，盡情跳舞，唱精靈的歌曲，稍後便離開此地。（她指著不同的精靈。）你去殺死啃食玫瑰花的蟲子；你去與蝙蝠宣戰並取其翅膀，為我的小精靈們製作外衣；你去趕走夜裡來此對我們嗚嗚叫的吵雜的貓頭鷹。現在，唱歌助我入睡吧，然後各自去忙，讓我好好休息。

（精靈們唱歌。）

精靈們： 你們這些舌尖分叉的蛇，臭鼬和甲蟲，莫要被看到；蟲子和蜥蜴，莫要惹禍出錯，切勿前來打擾我們的精靈皇后。

（提泰妮婭入睡。）

精靈： 任務達成，我們走吧！

（精靈們下。）

（奧布朗上，他將花朵的汁液塗在提泰妮婭闔起的眼皮上。）

奧布朗：你在甦醒之後的所見，便是你的真愛，務必愛他和
　　　　為他受苦難。不論是豬、或是貓、或是熊，待你醒來後出
　　　　現在你眼前，即是你唯一的愛。有卑劣之人靠近時，你便
　　　　要醒來。

（奧布朗下。赫米婭與拉山德上。）

拉山德：美麗的愛人，你在森林裡遊蕩之後略顯疲態。說實
　　　　話，我已經迷失了方向。倘若你覺得合適，赫米婭，我們
　　　　在此處休息，讓我們於此等待天明。

赫米婭：好的，拉山德，你去為自己找張床，我就以這個土
　　　　堆為枕頭。

拉山德：同一處可作我倆的枕頭，我們的心合而為一。

赫米婭：不，拉山德，為了我著想，親愛的，躺得離我遠一
　　　　點，切莫躺在我身旁。

拉山德：莫要誤解我，我的甜心！我言下之意是我的靈魂與
　　　　你合而為一，所以讓我酣睡在你身旁吧。我既這樣躺臥
　　　　入眠，赫米婭，必不會違背我的誓言。

赫米婭：拉山德，你果真是口齒伶俐。請原諒我的無禮和自
　　　　尊，赫米婭絕對無意疑心拉山德！但是我高尚的朋友，請
　　　　你躺得離我遠一點，你我男未婚、女未嫁，孤男寡女保持
　　　　距離才是上策。所以，與我保持距離吧——晚安了，體貼
　　　　的好友，但願我們的愛情此生不渝。

拉山德：倘若我結束了愛情，願我生命也就此告終！我以此
　　　　為床，但願你能安睡，好好休息！

赫米婭：我全心全意祝福你！

（他們入睡。帕克上。）

帕克：我已踏遍了森林各處，卻未能找到雅典人，讓我將這花朵的愛情汁液倒入他的眼中。（*他遇上了拉山德與赫米婭。*）寂靜的夜晚！是何人在此？他身穿雅典服飾！此即陛下所指的憎恨那雅典少女之人，而那少女也在此，躺在潮濕又骯髒的地上酣睡。美麗的靈魂！她不該與此人並肩躺臥，這不合禮法。（*他將花朵的汁液塗抹在拉山德的眼皮上。*）蠢貨！我在你的眼皮上施盡了這所有的魔法，待你醒來之時，就讓愛情使你機警得難以入眠吧。等我離開之後你再醒來，我這就去向奧布朗回報。

（*帕克下。狄密特律斯與海麗娜奔跑而上。*）

海麗娜：留下來──即便你殺了我也無妨，親愛的狄密特律斯。

狄密特律斯：我告訴你，請你離開！莫要再如此窮追不捨。

海麗娜：喔，難道你要丟下我獨自在黑暗中嗎？莫要離去。

狄密特律斯：你自行在此承受風險，我將獨自離去。

（*狄密特律斯下。*）

海麗娜：我已追趕得上氣不接下氣。倘若我再繼續，必定會顏面盡失。不論躺臥在何處，赫米婭都是幸福滿溢，因她受到祝福，擁有美麗的雙眼。她的眼睛並未因泛淚而閃著光芒；倘若如此，我的眼睛會比她的更美。不、不，我醜陋有如野熊，因野獸見著我就嚇得逃竄；所以難怪狄密特律斯亦如野獸一般，見到我就跑。（*她看到拉山德在熟睡。*）但這是何人在此？拉山德，躺在地上！是死了，或是熟睡？我沒看到鮮血，也沒有傷口。拉山德，倘若你活著，好先生，醒一醒吧。

拉山德（*醒來見到海麗娜*）：我願為你赴湯蹈火！親愛的海麗

娜！我終於看透了你的心思！狄密特律斯何在？喔，那卑鄙的名字！那個名字應該被我一劍刺死！

海麗娜：莫出此言，拉山德。他愛你的赫米婭又何如？美麗的赫米婭仍然深愛著你，你是該開心了。

拉山德：和赫米婭在一起開心？此刻我後悔與她共處的所有無聊時刻，我並不愛赫米婭！我愛的是海麗娜。誰會不願意拿烏鴉交換一隻白鴿？唯有理智才能動搖男人的心，而理智說你才是值得我愛的女子。至今年少的理智尚未成熟，然而如今我發覺赫米婭並非我的所愛，理智引導我與你深情相望，我在你眼裡看到愛情最豐富的書本中的愛情故事。

海麗娜：你何以如此嘲弄我？我做了什麼應得如此就待遇？狄密特律斯未曾給過我好臉色看，年輕人，這還不夠嗎？現在我還得聽你消遣我？再見！我必須聲明，在此之前，我認為你是個紳士。喔，我才被一個男人拒絕，現在又被另一個冷嘲熱諷！

（海麗娜下。）

拉山德（對熟睡中的赫米婭）：留下吧，赫米婭，莫要再接近拉山德！我彷彿吃了太多的甜食，見到你我就反胃作嘔。我憎惡你，現在我是全心愛著海麗娜，甘願作她的騎士！

（拉山德下。赫米婭醒來。）

赫米婭（驚嚇）：救我，拉山德！喔，把在我身上爬的這條蛇拿開！喔！我已然清醒！好可怕的噩夢啊！拉山德，你瞧，我嚇得全身發抖，還以為有蛇要吞掉我的心臟──而你還面帶微笑地坐視不管。拉山德！怎麼，你走了嗎？拉山德！你在何處？說話啊，倘若你能聽見。說話！我差點要

135

因驚嚇而昏厥了。毫無回應？那我確定你不在附近了，若未能儘快找到你，我就要死在這兒了。

（赫米婭下。）

第三幕

●第一場─────────────────────────P. 045

（昆斯、斯納格、波頓、弗魯特、斯諾特與斯塔佛林上，走進森林裡看到提泰妮婭躺著熟睡。）

波頓：全到齊了嗎？

昆斯：正好準時，這是我們綵排的絕佳地點。這個綠色區域就是我們的舞台，那裡的樹叢則是後台。我們來排演一次，如同我們將在公爵面前表演的一般。

波頓：皮特昆斯！

昆斯：你有何話要說，波頓？

波頓：在這皮拉姆斯與提絲比的喜劇中，有幾處是做不到的。首先，皮拉姆斯必須拔劍自戕，在場的女士們不會想看到這樣的東西！你的看法如何？

斯塔佛林：我認為台詞和動作皆已交代了情節，我們還是刪去殺戮的橋段吧。

波頓：那倒不然！我有個計畫能使一切順利進行。寫一段開場白讓我念出來，在開場白中聲明我們持劍決不傷害生靈，就說皮拉姆斯並非真的被殺死，只是要再確保──說我是扮演皮拉姆斯，而非真正的皮拉姆斯，我其實是織工波頓，如此大家便能輕鬆以待了。

昆斯：甚好！我們就寫這麼一段開場白吧。

斯諾特：女士們不會害怕獅子嗎？

斯塔佛林：我知道我會害怕！

波頓：你此言有理，有獅子出現在女士們面前，她們必會嚇得花容失色！此事我們應該三思。

斯諾特：我們必須聲明他並非真的獅子！

波頓：不，你必須說出他的名字，並且在獅子的頸部以上露出他的半張臉。他應該親口說出這樣的話：「女士們」或是「美麗的女士們，我誠摯希望你們──」不，或許應該這樣說：「我請求你們」或是「我懇請你們莫要害怕！倘若你們認為我是一隻獅子，那你們就錯了。不，我並不是獅子，我和其他人一樣皆為人類。」然後再讓他說出自己的名字，坦白地告訴大家他是細木工匠斯納格。

昆斯：好的，就這麼辦，但是還有兩個問題。首先，我們要如何引月光照進房間內？你們都知道，皮拉姆斯和提絲比是在月光下相會的。

斯諾特：在我們預定要演出話劇的當晚會有月光嗎？

波頓：去查查日曆！看看幾時會有月光。

昆斯（取出日曆）：是的，當晚會有月光。

波頓：哎呀，那就在我們表演的房間內，留一扇敞開的窗戶吧，月光會從窗戶照進來。

昆斯：是的，有人可以打扮成月仙子，他就說他代表月亮。然後還有一件事：我們需要房間內有一面牆，故事是說皮拉姆斯和提絲比透過牆上的一個洞在說話。

斯諾特：根本不可能搬動一面牆。你意下如何，波頓？

第三幕

第一場

137

波頓：就讓我們其中一人扮演那面牆吧。他可以在身上塗灰泥或一些泥巴，打扮成一面牆。讓他像這樣張開手指頭，皮拉姆斯和提絲比就能透過那個洞低聲説話了。

昆斯：倘若此法可行，那一切就應刃而解了。來，坐吧，所有母親的兒子，開始綵排各自的角色。皮拉姆斯，你先開始，待你説完台詞之後就去後台，其他人也一樣。

（帕克上，台上的眾人看不見他。）

帕克（竊語）：這些小丑何以在如此靠近精靈皇后酣眠之處？什麼——一齣話劇？我來當觀眾，或許也能在必要時當個演員。

昆斯：説話吧，皮拉姆斯。提絲比，你去準備。

波頓（扮演皮拉姆斯）：提絲比，甜美有如花朵的芬芳，你的氣息亦然。但是你聽！有聲音！你在此稍候，我未幾即會回到你面前。

（波頓下，進入樹叢中。）

帕克（竊語）：我從未見過有比他更奇怪的皮拉姆斯！

（帕克下，尾隨著波頓。）

弗魯特：現在換我説話嗎？

昆斯：是的，你必須説話，你要知道他是聽到聲音前去一探究竟，不久即會返回。

弗魯特（扮演提絲比）：皮拉姆斯，如紅玫瑰似地白皙，年輕、俊美，如同最真誠的馬兒一般誠摯，我將至「尼尼之墓」與你會面。

昆斯（情緒激動）：是「尼諾斯之墓」，先生！而且尚未到你説這句台詞的時機，那是你要回應皮拉姆斯的話。皮拉姆斯，你必須進來，你錯過了尾白的提示，你聽到「最真誠的馬兒」就該上台了。

（帕克隨著波頓上，波頓戴著一個驢子頭卻渾然不自知。）

波頓：倘若我俊美白皙，提絲比，我會只屬於你一人。

昆斯（被驢子頭嚇到）：喔，有怪物！我們遇鬼了！救命啊！

（昆斯、弗魯特、斯諾特、斯納格與斯塔弗林下，獨留波頓與帕克。）

帕克：我會跟隨著你們。我們繞著沼澤、樹叢和森林兜圈子，有時我是一匹馬，有時是一隻狗、一隻豬、一隻無頭的熊，有時是一團火。我會發出馬嘶、狗吠、豬叫、熊吼，也會燃燒，如同馬、狗、豬、熊、火一般。

（帕克下。）

波頓：他們何以倉皇逃開？這是他們在捉弄我，蓄意使我害怕。

（斯諾特再上。）

斯諾特：喔，波頓，你變身了，我在你身上看到什麼？（指著驢子頭。）

波頓：你看到什麼？你看到和你自己一樣的驢子頭，是嗎？

（斯諾特下。昆斯再上。）

昆斯：祝福你，波頓！你變了。

（昆斯下。）

波頓：我明白他們的用意了，他們是想嘲弄我，竭盡所能地嚇唬我。但是不論他們怎麼做，我決不離開此處。我會在此來回踱步，我也會唱歌，讓他們知道我並不害怕。（波頓唱歌。）「有著橘色喙的黑鳥，唱起歌兒如此真誠的知更鳥，鷦鷯的小尾羽──」

139

提泰妮婭（醒來）：是何天使將我從我的花床上喚醒？

波頓（仍在唱歌）：「雀鳥、麻雀和雲雀，灰色的鳥兒歌聲如此
樸實──」

提泰妮亞：再唱一次，高尚的凡人啊，我的耳朵聽到你的歌聲
便充滿歡愉，我的眼睛看到你俊美的相貌亦是喜悅滿盈。
關於你的一切皆令我感動，我發誓我對你是一見鍾情！

波頓：我倒認為你並無理由如此，女士。但是老實說，這年頭
理智和愛情並非好友，遺憾的是人們不再將二者聯想在一
起。這只是個小玩笑話！

提泰妮婭：你不僅相貌俊美，亦是絕頂聰明。

波頓：我二者皆非！但是倘若我夠聰明得以走出這座森林，那
我就心滿意足了。

提泰妮婭：不！不論你是否願意，你都得留在此處。我並非一
般的精靈，夏天是我的僕人，而且我是真心愛你。所以，跟
我走吧！我會賜予你精靈們，讓他們下海打撈珠寶給你；
他們會於你睡在花朵上時歌唱，而我會取走你的凡人特
質，好讓你成為飄逸如空氣一般的精靈。豌豆花！蛛網！飛
蛾！芥子！

（豌豆花、蛛網、飛蛾與芥子上。）

豌豆花：我在此。

蛛網：在此。

飛蛾：在此。

芥子：在此。

全體：要我們前去何處？

提泰妮婭：對這位紳士要和善有禮，在他面前蹦蹦跳跳，在
　　他視線之內躍動；給他吃杏實和野莓，還有紫色的葡萄和
　　綠色的無花果；給他蜜蜂所採集的蜂蜜；至於蠟燭，就用
　　蜜蜂腿上的蜂蠟，以螢火蟲的眼睛來點燃。為我的愛人指
　　路，領他就寢和起身；取五彩蝴蝶的翅膀，當成扇子來喚
　　醒他沉睡的雙眼。好好照顧他，精靈們！務必無微不至。

豌豆花：凡人萬歲！

蛛網：萬歲！

飛蛾：萬歲！

芥子：萬歲！

波頓：你們好！請問貴姓大名？

蛛網：蛛網。

波頓：我希望能進一步認識你，好蛛網先生。倘若我割傷了手
　　指，我會需要你。(對豌豆花:)請問你的大名，好先生？

豌豆花：豌豆花。

波頓：請代我問候令堂豆莢太太，以及令尊豆莢先生。(對芥
　　子:)請問你的大名，先生？

芥子：芥子。

波頓：好芥子先生，我對你甚是熟稔。我配著烤牛肉，吃過許
　　多你的家人。告訴你，你的親戚們使得我眼眶泛淚！我們必
　　須更常見面。

提泰妮婭(對精靈們)：來吧，服侍他，領他前去我的寢宮。縛
　　住我愛人的舌頭，悄然無聲地帶他去。

(全體下。)

（奧布朗上，走到森林裡的另一處。）

奧布朗：不知提泰妮婭是否已然甦醒；倘若如此，我想知道她第一眼看到的是什麼，此刻必定使她神魂顛倒。（帕克上。）我的信差來了。情況如何，瘋精靈？你又如何惡作劇了？

帕克：尊夫人愛上了一個怪物。在她的寢宮附近，趁著她熟睡之時，我看到一群工人──在雅典擺攤子為求溫飽而努力工作的粗魯人，他們聚在一起綵排話劇，預備在忒修斯的婚禮當天演出。其中最愚蠢又膚淺的一個扮演皮拉姆斯一角，他離開舞台走進了樹叢裡，此時我逮到機會捉弄他；我在他肩膀上放了一個驢子頭。不久，他的提絲比呼喚他，於是他在這尾白的提示下離開樹叢，回到覆滿青草的舞台。其他演員看到他戴著驢子頭，因害怕而四下逃竄，如同躲避獵人的野雁一般。他們起身嘎嘎大叫，一面尖叫、一面逃跑，有一個還摔倒了，大喊「殺人了！」他們的感覺不敏銳，驚恐的情緒倒是很強烈；他們開始以為樹叢和荊棘抓住了他們的衣服。我引領他們因驚慌和困惑而逃跑，留下可愛的、變身之後的皮拉姆斯站在那兒。就在那個當下，提泰妮婭正好醒來，愛上了一頭驢子。

奧布朗：這結果比我預期的更好！但你是否照著我的吩咐，用愛情的汁液塗在那雅典人的眼皮上？

帕克：是的，這我也照辦了。那個雅典女人正好在他身旁，所以待他醒來之時，他必定第一眼就會見到她。

（狄密特律斯與赫米婭上。）

奧布朗：躲起來！那個雅典人來了。

帕克：但我遇見的不是那個人！

狄密特律斯：你何以對真心愛你之人如此殘忍？你對待仇敵才應該如此冷酷啊！

赫米婭：我已耐心待你至此，但是我應該待你更刻薄才是，因你給了我咒罵的理由。你是否趁著拉山德熟睡時殺了他？你是否踩在他的血泊之中？倘若如此，你也應該拿刀殺了我。太陽再忠誠也比不上他對我，難道他會丟下我獨自睡在森林裡？我寧可相信我能在地上挖個洞，讓月光透進來。想必是你殺了他！你生得一副殺人兇手的樣貌——死氣沉沉、令人毛骨悚然。

狄密特律斯：被害人看似死亡，我也應為如此；你的殘酷如利刃刺中我的心！然而你這殺人兇手，卻看似清朗夜晚的金星一般閃耀。

赫米婭：拉山德究竟出了何事？他身在何處？喔，好狄密特律斯，將他交予我吧。

狄密特律斯：我寧可將他的遺體丟去餵我的狗。

赫米婭：走啊，你這隻狗！你逼迫我超越了我耐心的極限。難道你真的殺了他？倘若如此，你便不配被稱作人類！喔，告訴我實話，就當是為了我！你是否趁著他熟睡時殺了他？喔，你可真勇敢啊！一條蛇的劣行也不過如此！是啊，這是蛇下的毒手！未曾見過如你一般歹毒的蛇！

狄密特律斯：你是在我身上虛耗你的憤怒，我並未殺死拉山德。據我所知，他並沒有死。

赫米婭：那就請你告訴我他安然無恙。

狄密特律斯：倘若我告訴你，我能得到什麼好處？

赫米婭：你的禮物就是：再也見不到我。我要走了，不再與我憎恨的你同在此處。無論他是死或活，你都不會再見到我。

（赫米婭下。）

狄密特律斯：在她如此盛怒的情緒之下，我再跟著她也是徒勞，不如我在這兒待一會兒稍事休息吧。

（狄密特律斯就地躺臥而睡。）

奧布朗（對帕克）：你做了什麼？你犯了滔天大錯，將愛情汁液塗在真愛的眼皮上！如今真愛已變得虛假——而非虛假的愛情變為真！

帕克：那就由命運決定吧，因儘管有一人忠於他的愛情，但是更有百萬的人違背一個又一個的誓言。

奧布朗：快去，速度要比風更快，前去尋覓雅典的海麗娜。找一個不斷為愛而深深嘆息的女子，她已然心碎滿地。使些把戲帶她來此地，待她到附近我再下點魔咒在他的眼皮上。

帕克：我這就去、我這就去，瞧瞧我的速度，比弓射出箭還要迅速。

（帕克下。奧布朗將汁液塗在狄密特律斯的眼皮上。）

奧布朗：紫色染料點綴的花啊，當丘比特射出他的箭，沉入此人的眼睛裡面；當他的真愛經過眼前，讓她閃耀映入他的眼簾，如同夜空的金星一般耀眼。

（帕克再上。）

帕克：我們精靈大軍的將領，海麗娜已來到此地。那個男子被我錯認，他將在你眼前追求他的愛人。天哪，這些可真是愚蠢的凡人！

奧布朗：躲開。他們的嘈雜聲音，可能會將狄密特律斯吵醒。

帕克：那這兩人會同時追求她吧，我們旁觀必定很有趣。看著凡人白費力氣，我向來都看得笑嘻嘻。

（奧布朗與帕克躲開。拉山德與海麗娜上。）

拉山德：你何以認定我是在嘲弄你？沒人會在惡作劇之時哭泣。你瞧──我在啜泣！含淚立下的誓言，才是最真誠的。我對你的感情何以被你看作虛假？我戴著愛情的臂章，證明我的感情不假。

海麗娜：你說得愈多，就是撒愈大的謊；你對赫米婭也說了相同的話！難道你會離開她？將你對她和對我的誓言，置於天平的兩端；兩者等同重量──皆如花言巧語一般輕。

拉山德：我對她許下諾言時並不理智。

海麗娜：你現在違背那些諾言，亦非理智之舉。

拉山德：狄密特律斯愛的是赫米婭，不是你。

狄密特律斯（醒來見到海麗娜）：海麗娜，我的女神！你完美有如天仙下凡！要我如何比擬你的雙眸？用水晶來比擬亦相形見絀。你的雙唇有如櫻桃，最適合一親芳澤！當我看到你的手，高巍山頭的皚皚白雪亦顯得烏黑。喔，就是現在，讓我親吻你那白皙的手吧！

海麗娜（對兩人）：喔，好可惡！現在你倆都在嘲弄我了。倘若你們心地善良又識點禮節，就莫要如此待我；你們想必是憎恨我才會如此戲弄我。倘若你們是男人，你倆確實看似男人，你們就不該用虛偽的承諾和讚美來污蔑一位淑女！我知道你倆都愛赫米婭。這個遊戲還真有男子氣概啊──嘲弄一個可憐的少女，惹她哭泣！紳士是不會這麼做的。

拉山德：你不厚道，狄密特律斯，切莫這麼做。你愛的是赫米婭，你我都心裡有數。在此，我懷著善意、真心實意地宣布，我放棄追求她了，她是屬於你的，現在也請你放棄追求海麗娜。我愛她，對她的愛將至死不渝！

海麗娜：傻瓜也不會如此多費唇舌！

狄密特律斯：拉山德，留著你的赫米婭吧。倘若我曾愛過她，那份愛亦早已消逝，她在我心中只是個過客，如今我心已在海麗娜身上找到歸宿。

拉山德：海麗娜，事實並非如此。

狄密特律斯：莫要評論你不知情之事，你說的話可能危及你的身家安全，你可能必須付出代價。瞧瞧是誰來了——是你的愛人。

（赫米婭上。）

赫米婭：黑夜剝奪了視力，使聽力更為敏銳；在黑夜損及視力的同時，亦使得聽力倍增。我並非透過雙眼找到你，是我的耳朵領我來此，拉山德，你何以那般地拋下我？

拉山德：我對另一位美麗女子的愛催促我離開，我有何理由留下來？

赫米婭：是什麼愛竟然從我身邊偷走了你？

拉山德：我對美麗的海麗娜的愛，她使黑夜比繁星更加明亮。你找我有何事？你難道看不出來，我離開你是因為我厭惡你嗎？

赫米婭：你此話並未當真！這不可能是真的。

海麗娜：看啊，她亦是他們的同謀！現在我知道他們三人聯手戲弄我！害人精赫米婭！最忘恩負義的朋友！儘管我們事事共享，你還如此待我？我們情同姐妹啊！我們經常膩在一起！每當時光飛逝，迫使我們不得不分別，你我還會同感不捨。難道你忘了我們求學時期的友誼嗎？赫米婭，我們坐在同一張椅墊上，用同一個刺繡花樣繡著同一朵花；我們唱著同一首歌，你我同調，彷彿我們的雙手、側影、聲音和心靈皆合而為一。我們好似生長在同一根莖梗上的兩顆可口的野莓，你我曾經二人同心！如今你不顧我們的舊情，竟與兩個男人聯手嘲笑你可憐的朋友？這可不是友善之舉——女孩兒們不應如此。雖然只有我心受傷，但是其他女子亦會認同我的說法。

赫米婭：我很訝異你如此激動。我並未嘲笑你，似乎是你在嘲笑我。

海麗娜：難道你並未差遣拉山德，前來讚美我的雙眼和面容嗎？你不也差遣你的另一個愛慕者狄密特律斯，喚我為女神和天仙下凡嗎？他何以對他憎惡之人如此說話？拉山德又何以說他並不愛你？若非是聽你的指使，他何以會向我告白示愛？我或許不如你貌美，抑或是不如你幸運——擁有這麼多人的愛慕，但是像我這般的人，如此不幸、滿懷愛意卻又不被愛——應該被人同情，而非被人厭惡。

赫米婭：我不明白你此言為何意。

海麗娜：是啊，繼續演戲，用你虛偽的哀傷神情，趁我轉身時對我扮鬼臉，彼此相視眨眼。繼續戲弄我吧，這段軼事將會永留青史。倘若你還有同情心、仁慈或禮儀，就不該如此對待我。再會了，這有一部分要怪我自己，我就以離開來結束這一切吧。

拉山德：留下來，溫柔的海麗娜。聽我說，我的愛人、我的生命、我的靈魂，美麗的海麗娜！

海麗娜（語氣尖酸地）：喔，演得可真好！

赫米婭：親愛的，莫要如此嘲弄她。

拉山德：你的威脅有如她的禱告一般地薄弱。海麗娜，我愛你，我以我的性命起誓。

狄密特律斯：我說我愛你的次數多過於他。

拉山德：既然你這麼說，那就證明吧。

狄密特律斯（準備決鬥）：我樂意奉陪。

赫米婭（抓住拉山德）：拉山德，這一切究竟有何意義？

拉山德：走開，你這貓猻！放開我，否則我要當你是條蛇似地甩開你。

赫米婭：你何以變得如此無禮？你為何變成這樣，親愛的愛人？

拉山德：親愛的愛人？走開，令我厭惡的東西！

赫米婭：這可是玩笑話？

海麗娜：是啊，的確如此，你亦然。

拉山德：狄密特律斯，我仍要向你挑戰，我會對你言而有信。

狄密特律斯：但願我能將此言寫成白紙黑字，我不相信你說的話。

拉山德：什麼？難道要我傷害她、毆打她、殺死她？雖然我憎惡她，但是我不會傷她半根汗毛。

赫米婭：什麼？你還能傷得我更深嗎？憎惡我！為什麼？這是怎麼回事，我的愛人？我不是赫米婭嗎？你不是拉山德嗎？我和昨天的我並無兩樣；你昨晚還愛著我，為何棄我而去？喔，但願眾神助我，這一切都沒有發生！你此話可當真？

拉山德：是的，我以性命起誓！我不想再見到你了，所以你莫再期望、質問和懷疑。你可以確定，沒有比此言更真誠的話語；這決非戲言，我確實憎惡你、深愛海麗娜。

赫米婭：喔，不！（對海麗娜：）你這小偷！你這愛情的竊賊！你是否在夜裡摸黑前來，偷走了我愛人的心？

海麗娜：好吧，我明白了！難道你恬不知恥嗎？你非要從我溫柔的舌頭扯下憤怒的回應嗎？可恥、可恥！你這虛偽的傀儡！

赫米婭：「傀儡」？原來這遊戲是如此這般，現在我知道她是如何贏得他的心了。她早已言明她的個子比我高；你在他眼裡變得這麼高，是因為我太矮小嗎？我是多矮小，你這彩繪的五朔節花柱？說啊！我是多矮小？我並未矮到手指甲觸碰不到你的眼睛！

海麗娜：兩位紳士，雖然你們嘲弄我，但是莫要讓她傷害我。我沒有打鬥的天分，我確實是個淑女，切莫讓她毆打我。或許你們認為，因她是比我矮一截的女子，所以我能與她一較高下。

赫米婭：「矮一截」？聽聽她的鬼話！

海麗娜：請你莫要對我如此苛刻，我一向愛你，赫米婭，我未曾對你有過不公。我唯一做過的事，就是愛上狄密特律斯，而將你們要在這座森林裡私會的事告訴了他，他才尾隨你們來此。出於愛，我亦尾隨他，但是他要我離開。現在，倘若你願意讓我安靜地離開，我會將我愚蠢的愛還予雅典，不再對你亦步亦趨。放開我，此乃現在我唯一的要求。

赫米婭：你儘管走啊！有何事阻攔你？

海麗娜：我遺留的愚蠢的心。

赫米婭：什麼？留給拉山德嗎？

海麗娜：留給狄密特律斯。

拉山德：莫要害怕，她不會傷害你的，海麗娜。

海麗娜：喔，當她憤怒之時，她的力大無窮！她在求學時期便是個悍婦；她或許看起來嬌小，但是她凶狠潑辣。

赫米婭：又說我「嬌小」！不是「矮一截」就是「嬌小」！（對兩個男人：）你們何以讓她這般說話？讓我教訓她！

拉山德（拉住赫米婭）：走開，你這侏儒、你這鼠輩、你這小珠子、你這小橡實！

狄密特律斯（對拉山德）：你對海麗娜太過於慇勤，而她並不想要你，離她遠一點。莫要與她同一陣線；倘若你對她表現出一丁點的愛意，我就要你付出代價。

拉山德：你有膽就隨我來，我們來一較高下，看看誰才更有資格擁有海麗娜。

狄密特律斯：隨我來！不，我與你同往！

（拉山德與狄密特律斯下，準備決鬥。）

赫米婭（對海麗娜）：這一切都是你的錯。（海麗娜退開。）不，莫要後退。

海麗娜：我不信任你，我不想留在這兒，你對我動手是速度比較快，但是我的腿長，跑得更快。

（海麗娜下。）

赫米婭：我深感驚愕，已經無言以對。

（赫米婭下。）

奧布朗（對帕克）：這又是另一次犯錯，抑或是你蓄意而為？

帕克：相信我，陛下，是我犯了錯。你不是吩咐我要找身穿雅典服飾之人嗎？所以在雅典人的眼皮上塗了汁液又豈能怪我？目前為止我很慶幸自己的所為——看著他們相爭真是樂趣無窮。

奧布朗：如今那些人想尋覓打鬥地點。你快去，帕克，使夜變得漆黑，引領這雙死對頭迷失方向暫不狹路相逢。你分別用對方的聲音各自挑釁，用拉山德的聲音激怒狄密特律斯，然後再用狄密特律斯的聲音惹惱拉山德；往復地誤導他們，直到他們落入如死亡一般的熟睡中，接著再用此汁液塗在拉山德的眼皮上。（他將花朵交予帕克。）這有導正過錯的效力，使他的眼睛恢復從前之所能視。待他清醒之後，這一切的憤怒會彷彿夢境一般。這四個有情人會回到雅典，他們將永世感覺與今夜密切相關。在你置辦此事之際，我會去找我的皇后，懇求她將那印度男孩交予我，同時我會解除她對那驢子的愛情魔咒。

帕克：我的精靈國王陛下，此事必須速速辦妥，因時已幾近天明，在夜裡出沒的鬼魂們，現在都要返回他們爬滿蟲子的長眠之所了，深恐白晝會顯露出他們的羞愧，他們遠離光明，只會在漆黑的夜裡外出活動。

奧布朗：但我們是精靈，而非鬼魂。我經常在晨光中跳舞，也看過太陽從海平面升起。但是你此言依然在理，莫要耽擱，我們可在天亮前辦妥此事。

（奧布朗下。）

帕克：上上下下，我會引領他們上上下下。田野村鎮之人對我都畏懼有加；頑皮鬼，引領他們上上下下。有一個來了。

（拉山德上。）

拉山德：你在何處，驕傲的狄密特律斯？快快回話。

帕克（模仿狄密特律斯的聲音）：我乃在此，惡徒，我的劍已出
　　鞘，準備就緒。你在何處？

拉山德：我即刻將與你決一高下。

帕克（假扮狄密特律斯）：那就隨我前往較平坦之處吧。

（拉山德下。狄密特律斯上。）

狄密特律斯：拉山德，再說話啊。你這懦夫，難道逃之夭夭
　　了？你是否藏在某個樹叢裡畏首畏尾？

帕克（模仿拉山德的聲音）：你這懦夫，你是在向繁星吹噓，對
　　著樹叢說你想決鬥，卻遲遲不敢現身？來啊，你這黃口小
　　兒，我要拿木棒好好教訓你一頓，要我拔劍相向，於我是一
　　種羞辱。

狄密特律斯：拉山德，你可在此？

帕克（模仿拉山德的聲音）：隨我的聲音過來，我們不在此處決
　　鬥。

（帕克與狄密特律斯下。拉山德再上。）

拉山德：他跑了，挑釁我隨他而去。當我趕赴他喚我之處，他
　　卻不見人影。那惡徒的速度比我快多了，我迅速尾隨，但是
　　他卻飛奔得更快。如今我已在黑暗的崎嶇之地迷失方向，
　　且讓我在此休息片刻。（他躺下。）來吧，溫柔的白晝，待你
　　展露灰白的微光之時，我會去尋狄密特律斯一決勝負。

（拉山德入睡。帕克與狄密特律斯再上。）

帕克（模仿拉山德的聲音）：喂、喂、喂！懦夫，你何以不現身？

狄密特律斯：你有膽就與我正面交鋒。你一直逃跑，沒有勇氣

出來面對我。你此刻身在何處？

帕克（*模仿拉山德的聲音*）：過來這兒，我在此處。

狄密特律斯：不，你在嘲弄我，倘若我在天明之時看到你的臉，我就要你付出代價！但是現在，你儘管去吧，我必須躺臥在這冰冷的床上，等待黎明的到來。

（*狄密特律斯躺下來入睡。海麗娜上。*）

海麗娜：喔，疲憊的夜！喔，漫長又難熬的夜！你就快快結束吧！升起啊，太陽，好讓我在天明時分趕回雅典，遠離這些憎惡我之人。睡眠有時會令憂愁的眼睛闔上，暫時帶我進入夢鄉吧。

（*海麗娜躺下來入睡。*）

帕克：只有三個？再來一個吧，兩兩成雙才能湊齊四個。她來了，心碎又悲傷。丘比特是個壞心眼的傢伙，竟如此逼得可憐的女子瘋狂。

（*赫米婭上。*）

赫米婭：未曾如此疲累，未曾如此心傷。更深露重，飽受荊棘摧殘，我已無力再往前走，就在此休息至破曉吧。倘若他們決鬥，但願上天保佑拉山德。

（*赫米婭躺下來入睡。*）

帕克：躺臥在地，沉沉睡去，我將在你的眼皮上塗抹這汁液。（*他將汁液塗抹在拉山德的眼皮上。*）當你醒來，你將感懷，見到真愛的眼睛，內心有多欣喜。有句俗話如此叮囑——有情人將終成眷屬——待你清醒之後必會清楚：人人皆有所屬，名花必能有主，男人將和他的另一半重逢，人人皆能心稱意如。

（*帕克下。*）

第四幕

● 第一場 ——————————————— P. 079

（在森林裡，拉山德、狄密特律斯、海麗娜與赫米婭皆躺臥在地熟睡。提泰妮婭與波頓、豌豆花、蛛網、飛蛾、芥子上，其他精靈們隨侍在側。奧布朗尾隨而上，其他人皆看不見他。）

提泰妮婭（對波頓）：來，坐在這花床上，讓我輕撫你美麗的臉龐。我要將玫瑰別在你光滑、柔順的頭髮上，親吻你迷人的大耳朵，我溫柔的喜悅。

波頓：豌豆花何在？

豌豆花：在此。

波頓：搔抓我的頭，豌豆花。蛛網先生何在？

蛛網：在此。

波頓：蛛網先生，帶著你的弓箭，殺死花朵上的那紅尾蜜蜂，將其蜜囊取來給我，小心莫要弄破了，否則你會全身沾滿蜂蜜。芥子先生何在？

芥子：在此。

波頓：將你的手借給我，芥子先生。也請你莫要再鞠躬了，先生。

芥子：你有何吩咐？

波頓：只是想請你給我抓個癢，好先生。我得去找個理髮師，先生，因我覺得我臉上的毛太濃密了。我是這麼一頭敏感的驢子，倘若毛惹得我發癢，我就得抓個癢。

提泰妮婭：你想聽點音樂嗎，我的愛人？

波頓：我熟諳音樂的聆賞，那就來點樂器演奏吧。

提泰妮亞：那你想吃點什麼？

波頓：一袋乾草，或者我可以吃點燕麥。我想還是來點乾草好了，好吃的乾草、甜美的乾草，全天下最美味的食物。

提泰妮婭：我有個膽大的精靈，可以從松鼠儲藏的糧食中取來堅果給你。

波頓：我還是吃點乾豆子就好了。但是現在，莫要讓任何精靈前來打擾我，我突然感到睏倦。

提泰妮婭：那就睡吧，我會將你擁在懷中。精靈們，都退下。（精靈們下。）喔，我好愛你啊！

（波頓與提泰妮婭入睡。帕克上。）

奧布朗（走上前來）：歡迎你，帕克！你是否看到這甜蜜的景象？我如今開始同情她愚蠢的愛了。不久之前，我在森林裡遇見她，給這個可憎的蠢貨尋找甜美的花朵，我還為此與她起了爭執。她用鮮採的芳香花朵為他編織成花環，戴在他毛茸茸的頭上。美麗的小花蕊還含著露珠，彷彿在為自身所受的屈辱而傷心哭泣。當我將我的想法告知予她之時，她溫和地央求我莫要如此嘲弄她。接著我向她要了那個孩子，她隨即欣然答應將他交予我；一位精靈帶著他前去我在精靈王國的寢宮。現在我有了那個男孩，也該解除我施在她眼皮上的魔法了。好了，高尚的帕克，取走這個雅典人頭上的驢子頭吧。在其他人醒來之時，讓他也醒來。但願他們悉數返回雅典，忘卻這一夜發生過的所有事；讓他們視之為一場夢。但是首先，我要解救精靈皇后。（觸摸提泰妮婭的眼睛：）回復你原來的模樣，重拾你原有的眼光。這甜美的花蕾有能力可解除丘比特愛情之花的魔力；現在，醒來吧，我親愛的皇后！

提泰妮婭：我的奧布朗！我作了個奇怪的夢！我以為我愛上了一頭驢子！

奧布朗（指向波頓）：那即是你的愛人。

提泰妮婭：事情如何演變至此？喔，我見到他便滿心厭惡啊！

奧布朗：暫且冷靜。帕克，取下他的驢子頭。（帕克除去波頓肩上的驢頭。）提泰妮婭，命人演奏音樂吧。至於這五個凡人，就讓他們以為自己睡了一整夜。

提泰妮婭：讓我們用音樂對他們的睡眠施法。

奧布朗：演奏吧，音樂。來吧，我的皇后，握著我的手，撼動這些人安睡的大地。（音樂演奏。奧布朗與提泰妮婭共舞。）如今你我有如新朋友一般，明日午夜我們將在忒修斯公爵的府上翩然起舞。我們要賜福予這個家系的未來；在那兒有兩對情侶，將步入幸福的婚姻殿堂。

帕克：精靈國王，仔細聆聽：雲雀告知我們晨光將臨。

奧布朗：來，我的皇后，如同月亮一般，讓我們迅速地繞地飛行。

提泰妮亞：來，我的夫君，在我們飛行之時，告訴我今夜所發生之事。我何以在熟睡之際，被發現與這些凡人一齊躺臥在地？

（奧布朗、提泰妮婭與帕克下。號角聲響起。忒修斯、他的僕人們、希波呂忒與伊吉斯上。）

忒修斯：去吧，你們其中一人！去尋來那管理森林及其動物們之人；五朔節慶典已然結束，現在出發狩獵還嫌太早，放我的獵犬們去西邊的山谷。我叫你們去啊，尋來那管理森林之人。（一名僕人下。）（對希波呂忒：）我們也走吧，美麗的皇后。我們將在那山頂上聆聽音樂，聽著獵犬們的吠叫和回音的共鳴。

希波呂忒：我曾與海克力士一同在克里特島上的森林裡狩獵。他們用斯巴達的獵犬來獵熊，我未曾聽過那般悅耳的聲音！樹木、天空、水泉和鄰近的各地，全都一起回響。我未曾聽過那般的樂音！如此甜美的震耳欲聾！

忒修斯：我的獵犬亦為同一品種，有著喉部垂肉和沙黃色的毛皮。牠們的頭上掛著長長的耳朵，掃去了晨間的露珠；牠們的聲音有如鐘聲似地洪亮，各自相應成調。獵人的號角亦未能吹奏出更悅耳的嘷叫聲，待你親耳聞之便知。（他看到沉睡的凡人們。）但是你看！此乃何人？

伊吉斯：閣下，在此熟睡的是小女，還有拉山德和狄密特律斯。這是海麗娜，老奈達的女兒。不知他們何以同在此處。

忒修斯：無疑他們是早起觀看五朔節的慶典，想必是聽聞我們要來觀禮而專程前來會見。但是告訴我，伊吉斯，今日莫不是赫米婭要告知她的抉擇之日？

伊吉斯：正是，閣下。

忒修斯（對一名僕人）：去吧，請獵人們用號角聲喚醒他們。（一名僕人下。從舞台後方傳來一聲叫喊。號角聲響起。沉睡的人們醒來，跪在忒修斯面前。）早安，朋友們，情人節已經過去了，這些鳥兒們正開始配對了嗎？

拉山德：請求寬恕，閣下。

忒修斯：各位，請起身。（他們站起來。）（對拉山德與狄密特律斯：）我知道你倆是死對頭，何以在妒忌之餘還能並肩而睡、不畏懼會有危險？

拉山德：閣下，我仍是半睡半醒，自身亦深感詫異。然而，我發誓我無法確切說明我何以在此，因我相信——事實上，我知道——我是隨同赫米婭來到此處，我們計畫離開雅典，前去一個不受雅典律法約束之處——

伊吉斯：閣下，你已聽夠了！我懇求你，依據律法懲處他。倘若他倆私奔了，狄密特律斯，那就是欺騙你我之舉；你被你的妻子欺騙，而我被我的承諾欺騙——我早已承諾將她許配予你為妻。

狄密特律斯：閣下，海麗娜將他們的計畫告知予我，我在盛怒之下尾隨他們，海麗娜亦跟隨我。而今，我不知是何力量——總之是有某種力量——使我對赫米婭的愛意如同冰雪一般地消融，現在那只像是我兒時鍾愛某個玩具的記憶一般。此刻，我的愛、我的心和我所有的感情，僅屬於海麗娜一人。閣下，我在見到赫米婭之前，即已與她訂下婚約，但是我有如失心瘋似地背棄了她；如今我已恢復理智，我回到了她的身邊。現在我要她、愛她、也戀慕她，我會永世對她忠誠。

忒修斯：神仙眷侶們，你們很幸運地被我們找到了，稍後再向我說明來龍去脈。伊吉斯，我必須駁回你的請求，因未幾將在神殿裡，為這兩對愛侶與我們一同舉行婚禮。今晨的時光飛逝，我們暫且取消狩獵之行。隨我們返回雅典吧，諸位，讓我們三對新人並肩而立，這將會是一場喜悅的婚禮！來吧，希波呂忒。

（忒修斯、希波呂忒、伊吉斯與僕人們下。）

狄密特律斯：這些事似是遙遠山頭上的過往雲煙。

赫米婭：我用惺忪的睡眼看待這些事，萬物似乎皆是疊影。

海麗娜：我的想法亦如是。狄密特律斯已是屬於我，如同珍寶一般，但卻又不屬於我。

狄密特律斯：你確定我們都醒著嗎？我覺得我們似乎仍在酣睡和作夢。你認為公爵方才果真在此，命我們隨他而去嗎？

赫米婭：是的，還有我父親。

海麗娜：還有希波呂忒。

拉山德：而且他命我們隨他們前往神殿。

狄密特律斯：那就隨他而去吧，就讓我們沿途各自敘述我們的夢境。

（兩對愛侶下。）

波頓（*醒來*）：當我的尾白提示之時，請呼喚我，我會回答。我的下一句台詞是「最俊美的皮拉姆斯」。有人在嗎？皮特昆斯？修風箱工匠弗魯特？補鍋匠斯諾特？斯塔佛林？我的老天！他們丟下我一人在此熟睡！我做了個極不尋常的夢，就連我自己也無法解釋！我覺得我是──我認為我有──但凡試圖說明我的想法之人皆是傻瓜。沒有人的眼睛曾經聽過，沒有人的耳朵曾經看過，沒有人的手曾經嘗過，他的舌頭亦未曾想到過，他的心無法觸摸我的夢境。我會請皮特昆斯寫一首關於此一夢境的歌謠，就命名為「波頓之夢」，因這是個無底之夢，我將在話劇的末了為公爵獻唱。

（波頓下。）

●第二場 ──────────────────── P. 091

（昆斯、弗魯特、斯諾特與斯塔佛林上，走進皮特昆斯在雅典的住家。）

昆斯：你有差人去波頓的住處嗎？他是否回到家中？

斯塔佛林：尚未有他的音信，他想必是出事了。

弗魯特：倘若他不來，這場話劇就毀了，無法再繼續了，不是嗎？

昆斯：不可能繼續，全雅典再無他人比波頓更適合扮演皮拉姆斯。

弗魯特：我有同感，他是雅典最有才華的工匠。

昆斯：是的，也是長相最俊美的。他的聲音最是悅耳動聽！

（斯納格上。）

斯納格：各位師傅們，公爵已大駕親臨，還有更多的貴族方才新婚燕爾。倘若我們的話劇演得好，我們必能升官發財。

弗魯特：喔，波頓！他剛損失了餘生的每天六便士，這是他逃不過的命運。倘若公爵未能因他扮演皮拉姆斯而賞賜他一天六便士，那我寧可被絞死！這畢竟是他應得的啊。

（波頓上。）

波頓：我的朋友們何在？

昆斯：波頓！喔，美好的一天！喔，最開心的時刻！

波頓：各位師傅們，我意欲告訴你們我的奇遇，但是莫要問我關於他們的事！倘若我告訴你們，我就不是真正的雅典人了。等待適當的時機，我會讓你們知曉一切。

昆斯：說來聽聽吧，可愛的波頓。

波頓：我不會透露半句，只能說公爵即將親臨，快去準備好戲服，束好你們的鬍子！我們到宮殿會合，每個人都要按各自的角色打扮好；讓提絲比穿著乾淨的衣裳，還有別讓獅子修剪他的指甲，因它們必須露出來成為獅子的利爪。還有，最親愛的演員們，切莫食用洋蔥或大蒜，這是美好的喜劇，我們必須有芳香的口氣！莫再多說了，去吧，快去準備！

（全體下。）

第五幕

● 第一場 ——————————————————— P. 095

（忒修斯、希波呂忒、菲勞斯特萊特、貴族諸公與僕人們上，走進忒修斯在雅典的宮殿。）

希波呂忒：我的忒修斯，這幾個愛侶敘述的故事很奇怪。

忒修斯：奇怪得不甚真實，我不相信童話故事。愛侶和瘋子皆是激情充腦，擁有的幻想超乎冷靜理性之人可以理解。瘋子、有情人和詩人有許多共同點；瘋子看到的魔鬼之多，絕非廣闊的地獄所能容納——有情人的瘋狂亦不相上下，能在最平凡的臉上見到海倫（編注：世上最美的女人）的美貌。詩人的眼睛一轉，即可從天上看至凡間，再從凡間看至天上；他的想像能創造奇蹟，再用他的筆賦予其家世姓名等具體細節。想像力豐富即可變出此般的把戲！倘若你想像一些喜悅，就會相信這喜悅是有人帶來的；抑或是在夜裡想像出恐懼，樹叢即可輕易地變成一頭熊！

希波呂忒：但是他們敘述的故事皆相去無幾！他們的心智看見了同樣的幻覺，似乎不只是想像而已。

（拉山德、狄密特律斯、赫米婭與海麗娜上。）

忒修斯：那幾個愛侶們來了，充滿喜悅和幸福。祝你們開心，高尚的朋友們，但願喜悅和愛情的新時光與你們同在，永留在你們心中！

拉山德：您比我們更應得到祝福！

忒修斯：來吧，自晚餐後至就寢前的這段時間，我們有何話劇和歌舞可打發？來，菲勞斯特萊特，告訴我們！

（菲勞斯特萊特走上前來。）

第五幕

第一場

163

菲勞斯特萊特：是的，閣下。

忒修斯：説吧，你今晚準備了什麼餘興節目？有何話劇？有何音樂？倘若未有令人愉快之事，我們該如何打發這閒暇的時間？

菲勞斯特萊特（將一張紙交給忒修斯）：偉大的忒修斯，這是今晚帶來音樂或其他餘興表演，並為各位助興的名單，請選擇一個您最喜歡的。

忒修斯（念出名單）：「與人頭馬身怪物搏鬥，由一名雅典人彈奏豎琴和演唱。」這就敬謝不敏了。「參加宴會而酒醉之人的暴動，在盛怒之下攻擊歌手。」這是老掉牙的話劇，我早已看過。「三位繆思女神為學習之死而哀悼。」那是刻薄尖酸的諷刺之作，不適合在大喜之日表演。「年輕的皮拉姆斯與他的愛人提絲比冗長而乏味的短劇，一部悲劇的喜劇。」一部悲劇的喜劇？冗長而乏味的短劇？這可比喻為「熱的冰」，完全不成理。這是何意？

菲勞斯特萊特：倘若此話劇只有十個字，那就嫌太長了，閣下；文字正是使之冗長而乏味的主因，因整部劇中沒有半個好字眼！我尊貴的閣下，這是悲劇，因為皮拉姆斯在劇中自盡而亡。當我看到他們綵排之時，我必須承認此劇使我眼眶泛淚，但我是因捧腹大笑而生淚。

忒修斯：演員們是何方人物？

菲勞斯特萊特：全是雅典的勤奮工匠，在此之前未曾絞盡腦汁思考過什麼。他們是專程為了您的大喜之日而準備的。

忒修斯：那就要看個究竟了。

菲勞斯特萊特：不，我尊貴的閣下，這不適合您看。我已經看過了，根本不值得一看。

忒修斯：我非看此劇不可，因動機單純正面之舉是不可能出錯的。去吧，傳他們進來。各自就座吧，女士們。

（菲勞斯特萊特下。）

希波呂忒：我不願見到有人因自不量力而感到尷尬。

忒修斯：親愛的夫人，你不會見到此般的情景！

希波呂忒：但是他說此一話劇糟糕至極。

忒修斯：讓我們心存寬容，感謝這些演員們吧；真摯的人們出於善意之努力，於我而言意義非凡。

（菲勞斯特萊特再上。）

菲勞斯特萊特：閣下，演員們已準備就緒。

忒修斯：讓他們開始吧。

（號角聲響起。昆斯、波頓、弗魯特、斯諾特、斯納格與斯塔佛林上。）

昆斯（朗讀開場白）：倘若我們有所冒犯，我們亦是出於善意。展現我們單純的技藝，才是我們結尾的真正開始。我們並非來此取悅諸位，這不是我等真正的意圖；我們亦非來此全為了討諸位的歡心，讓你們同情這些演員們的處境。藉由他們的演出，諸位將可知道所有想知道之事。

忒修斯：這位朋友說話毫無道理可言。

拉山德：他的這段開場白念得有如乳臭未乾的少年，不知該在哪兒停止。這是個好教訓，閣下：光是用說的並不夠，還必須盡量說得有真實感。

希波呂忒：他說話像個孩子在吹笛，只發出聲音，但是全都混淆不清。

忒修斯：他這番話就像交纏的鐵鍊——沒有破損斷裂，但全都糾結在一起。接下來是何人？

昆斯（繼續開場白）：高尚的諸位，或許你們對此劇抱有疑慮，但是請繼續揣測，直到一切真相大白為止。倘若你們非知道不可，此人是皮拉姆斯，這位美人是提絲比。此人扮演的是牆，這對愛侶要透過他低語傳情。此人是扮演月光，各位必須知道這對愛侶是在月光下相約於尼諾斯之墓，在那兒傾訴愛意。這是嚇跑提絲比的獅子；在她逃竄之際，她的外衣掉落在地上，被獅子用他的血盆大口撕得破爛。皮拉姆斯尾隨而至，他是俊美的高個兒青年；他撿到他愛人提絲比的染血外衣，勇敢地用利刃刺進自己激動的胸口。躲在附近陰暗處的提絲比，拔出了他的匕首自刎而死。就讓獅子、月光、牆和這對愛侶，將這個故事娓娓道來吧。

忒修斯：我倒想知道獅子是否會說話。

狄密特律斯：我倒不會訝異，閣下。倘若許多驢子都會說話，一頭獅子說話亦是在理。

斯諾特（扮演牆）：在這場話劇中，我斯諾特是扮演其上有個洞的牆。皮拉姆斯與提絲比這對愛侶，經常透過這個洞私會低語訴情意。這灰泥和石塊可證明我正是牆，事實即是如此。

忒修斯：真正的牆開口能說得比他更好嗎？

狄密特律斯：我沒聽過如此聰明的牆在說話，閣下！

忒修斯：皮拉姆斯來了。安靜！

波頓（扮演皮拉姆斯）：喔，最黑暗的夜晚！喔，黑夜，當白晝不再之時總是如此地漆黑！喔，黑夜！喔，黑夜！哎呀、哎呀、哎呀！我深怕提絲比已然忘卻她的承諾。而你，喔，甜美又可愛的牆，阻隔在她父親的土地與我的之間，給我一個洞讓我看穿吧。（牆張開了他的手指。）謝謝你，牆，但願眾神保佑你！但是我看到什麼？我看不見提絲比啊。喔，詛咒你，邪惡的牆，你竟然欺騙我！

忒修斯：牆應該詛咒回去。

波頓：不，說真的，先生，他不該如此。「欺騙我」是提絲比尾白的提示，她此刻應該上場，我將透過牆見到她，你們稍

167

候便知，劇情將如我所言地發展。她來了。

弗魯特（扮演提絲比）：喔，牆，你經常聽見我因與我俊美的皮拉姆斯分隔而哭泣！我的嘴唇經常親吻你的石塊。

波頓（扮演皮拉姆斯）：我看見有個聲音！現在我要透過牆，看看我能否聽見我的愛人提絲比的面容。提絲比！

弗魯特（扮演提絲比）：我的愛人！我想你應該是我的愛人。

波頓（扮演皮拉姆斯）：我擁有你的真愛，至今仍對你忠貞不二。

弗魯特（扮演提絲比）：而我亦如是，直到眾神取我性命！

波頓（扮演皮拉姆斯）：喔，透過這卑劣牆上的洞親吻我吧。

弗魯特（扮演提絲比）：哎呀！我親吻的是牆上的洞，而非你的嘴唇。

波頓（扮演皮拉姆斯）：你能否即刻前往尼尼之墓與我相會？

弗魯特（扮演提絲比）：不論死活，我皆會準時赴約。

（波頓與弗魯特下。）

斯諾特（扮演牆）：我已扮好我的角色，任務已了，這牆即將下台一鞠躬。

（斯諾特下。）

希波呂忒：我未曾聽聞如此愚蠢的對白！

忒修斯：最好的演員們皆只是影子。倘若發揮想像力加以改變，最糟的亦不過如此。

希波呂忒：那想必是你的想像，而非他們的。

忒修斯：我們莫要貶低他們，就如他們所想的那般肯定他們吧，如此他們便是優秀的演員。瞧！有個人和一頭獅子來了。

斯納格（扮演獅子）：女士們，你們內心畏懼這地上最小的老鼠，此刻見到怒吼的野生獅子，大可全身震顫和發抖，但是要知道我細工木匠斯納格並非真的是獅子，我只是個人類。

忒修斯：最溫和良善的動物。

狄密特律斯：這是我見過最好的野獸！

斯塔佛林（扮演月光）：這燈籠乃是月光，而我即是月仙子。

忒修斯：這是最大的錯誤。此人應被放入燈籠之內，否則他何以是月仙子？

狄密特律斯：他想必是不敢太靠近蠟燭。

希波呂忒：我厭煩了這個月亮，但願他能快點西沉！

忒修斯：他似乎稍嫌遲鈍了點，但是基於禮貌，我們必須留下來看完。

狄密特律斯：安靜！提絲比來了。

（弗魯特再上。）

弗魯特（扮演提絲比）：此即古老的尼尼之墓。我的愛人何在？

斯納格（扮演獅子，怒吼）：吼！

（扮演提絲比的弗魯特匆忙逃跑，她的外衣掉落在地上，扮演獅子的斯納格用牙齒將之撕咬。）

狄密特律斯：吼得好，獅子！

忒修斯：跑得好，提絲比！

希波呂忒：照得好，月光！

（波頓上。斯納格下。）

狄密特律斯：皮拉姆斯來了。

拉山德：所以獅子才走了。

波頓（扮演皮拉姆斯）：美好的月亮，感謝你如陽光一般的光芒；感謝你大放光明，月亮，相信你定能將提絲比帶到我面前。但是且慢！喔，不！這是何等駭人的哀傷情景？眼睛，你是否看見？這怎麼可能？喔，美麗的雁鴨！喔，親愛的！你的外衣如此美麗──怎麼？沾染了鮮血？來吧，喔，可怕的眾神！切斷我的懸命之線！摧毀我！結束我！讓我死吧！

忒修斯：此種強烈的情感、摯愛好友之死，確實能使人神情哀傷。

希波呂忒：詛咒我的心，但我很是同情此人。

波頓（扮演皮拉姆斯）：喔，大自然，你何以創造獅子？有隻惡毒的獅子吞了我的愛人，她是──不、不──她曾是素來被疼愛與受人喝采的最美麗的女子。來吧，眼淚！毀了我！出鞘吧，劍，刺傷我！切去皮拉姆斯的左半側身體，那是他的心臟跳動之處。（他假裝用劍刺自己。）我死了，就這樣、就這樣、就這樣。現在我死了，現在我已逃離，我的靈魂飛上天際。舌頭，失去你的光芒！月亮，飛逝吧。（扮演月光的斯塔佛林下。）現在，死、死、死、死、死吧。

（扮演皮拉姆斯的波頓假裝死去。）

希波呂忒：月光何以在提絲比回來找尋她的愛人前就退場？

（扮演提絲比的弗魯特再上。）

忒修斯：她會藉由星光找到他。瞧！她來了，她的獨白是全劇的結尾。

希波呂忒：希望她能言簡意賅，不值得為這樣的皮拉姆斯說這麼多話。

拉山德：她那雙美麗的眼睛已經見到他了。

狄密特律斯：她在哭泣之餘說話了：

弗魯特（扮演提絲比）：睡著了嗎，我的愛人？怎麼，死了，我的白鴿？喔，皮拉姆斯，醒來！說話、說話啊！啞口無言？死了、死了？想必是墳上的黃土掩了你美麗的雙眼。這蒼白的嘴唇、這櫻紅的鼻子、這蠟黃的雙頰皆不復見，不復見！有情人們，與我一同悲泣！他的雙眼曾經青綠如韭蔥。喔，死亡，用蒼白如乳汁的雙手前來找我吧，將之浸於鮮血中。舌頭，莫再多說。來吧，帶來幸福的劍；來吧，利刃，使我的胸口浸於鮮血之中。（她假裝刺死自己。）現在，再見了，朋友們，提絲比的生命已然終了。再見、再見、再見！

（她假裝死去。）

忒修斯：月光和獅子皆離去埋葬亡者了。

狄密特律斯：是啊，牆亦然。

（波頓與弗魯特站起來。）

波頓：不，我向各位保證，他們的父親們已拆毀阻隔他們的牆。你們想看看收場白嗎？或者你們寧可聽我們跳舞？

忒修斯：請你們莫要再上演收場白，此劇毋需再多作解釋，切莫解釋。當劇中人物們死去之時，毋需責怪任何人。倘若筆者扮演皮拉姆斯，用提絲比的長襪絞死了自己，那就是一場無可挑剔的悲劇了。如此甚好，演得也非常好，但是來吧，讓我們看看你們的歌舞表演，別管什麼收場白了。（演員們跳舞，然後下。）午夜時鐘的指針已指向十二點鐘。愛侶們，就寢吧！幾乎要到精靈的時間了。我深怕因我們今晚熬夜遲遲不睡，我們明早會睡得太晚；此劇正好符合這一夜的緩慢步調。好友們，就寢吧！兩個星期之後，我們將再次會面，一同慶祝另一場盛宴。

（全體下。帕克帶著一把掃帚上。）

帕克：此刻飢餓的獅子怒吼，野狼對著月亮嗥叫；疲累的農夫們大夢周公，辛勞的工作已然終了。而今火光逐漸熄滅，貓頭鷹此刻的鳴叫聲，提醒滿心苦惱的人類，終有一天他必須了結此生。在夜裡的這個時分，墓穴皆會敞開大門，各自放出其內的亡魂，他們將在黑暗道路上滑行。我們精靈們恣意飛奔，追逐著月夜的閃耀光芒，我們逃離刺眼陽光的親吻，亦步亦趨跟隨黑暗倘佯。現在我們要玩耍，這歡樂的氣氛不容老鼠搞砸。我亦曾受命持掃帚來清掃，將灰塵掃至門後就再也見不著。

（奧布朗與提泰妮婭上，帶著他們的精靈們。）

奧布朗（對精靈們）：發出閃閃的微光，在微弱將滅的火堆旁，所有的妖精和精靈同歡，輕躍野玫瑰叢如鳥兒一般。跟著我唱這首歌曲，一起唱歌和跳舞──一、二、三！

提泰妮婭：讓音樂悠揚地響起，每個字都配上悅耳的樂音。手牽著手用精靈的優雅姿態，我們將高歌使此地福到樂來。

（奧布朗領著精靈們唱歌跳舞。）

奧布朗：此刻直至天明破曉之前，我們將隨心所欲悠遊在此屋內。我們要去探訪每位新娘和新郎，使每個房間皆是幸福蕩漾。祝福他們所生的孩子乖巧伶俐，但願他們永世財富享不盡。祈望這三對佳偶，皆能真心終身相守。造物之手的醜陋印記，他們的孩子將不會遭遇。用這神奇的精靈露水，賜福於這整座宮殿。精靈們在各個房間穿梭來回，為這美好之地帶來平靜況味。但願這宮殿的主人福氣滿門，永遠無病無憂休息養神。速速前去翩舞盡興，待破曉時分再來與我同行。

（全體下，獨留帕克。）

帕克：倘若我們這些演員們有所冒犯，請想著一切錯誤皆有轉圜：在這些幻夢出現之際，你們皆熟睡於此地，而此薄弱又愚蠢的主題，不過只是一個夢境。好觀眾，莫要急欲喝倒采；我們必將彌補過錯，請海涵！因我帕克向來誠實無欺，倘若我們終究能有此好運，躲過你們憤怒的批評言語，我們反錯為正未幾亦是必需，否則儘管給帕克加個欺詐罵名。所以祝福各位安睡入夢裡，倘若諸位視我為友，請將你們的手給我，帕克未幾即可改正悔過。

（帕克下。）

Literary Glossary ● 文學詞彙表

aside 竊語

一種台詞。演員在台上講此台詞時,其他角色是聽不見的。角色通常藉由竊語來向觀眾抒發內心感受。

■ Although she appeared to be calm, the heroine's **aside** revealed her inner terror.
雖然女主角看似冷靜,但她的**竊語**透露出她內在的恐懼。

backstage 後台

一個戲院空間。演員都在此處準備上台,舞台布景也存放此處。

■ Before entering, the villain impatiently waited **backstage**.
在上台前,壞人在**後台**焦躁地等待。

cast 演員;卡司陣容

戲劇的全體演出人員。

■ The entire **cast** must attend tonight's dress rehearsal.
全體演員必須參加今晚的正式排練。

character 角色

故事或戲劇中虛構的人物。

■ Mighty Mouse is one of my favorite cartoon **characters**.
太空飛鼠是我最愛的卡通**人物**之一。

climax 劇情高峰

戲劇或小說中主要衝突的結局。

■ The outlaw's capture made an exciting **climax** to the story.
逃犯落網成為故事中最刺激的**精彩情節**。

comedy 喜劇

有趣好笑的戲劇、電影和電視劇，並有快樂完美的結局。

■ My friends and I always enjoy a Jim Carrey **comedy**.
　我朋友和我總是很喜歡金凱瑞演的**喜劇**。

conflict 戲劇衝突

故事主要的角色較量、勢力對抗或想法衝突。

■ *Dr. Jekyll and Mr. Hyde* illustrates the **conflict** between good and evil.
　《變身怪醫》描述善惡之間的**衝突**。

conclusion 尾聲

解決情節衝突的方法，使故事結束。

■ That play's **conclusion** was very satisfying. Every conflict was resolved.
　該劇的**結局**十分令人滿意，所有的衝突都被圓滿解決。

dialogue 對白

小說或戲劇角色所說的話語。

■ Amusing **dialogue** is an important element of most comedies.
　有趣的**對白**是大多喜劇中重要的元素之一。

drama 戲劇

故事，通常非喜劇類型，特別是寫來讓演員在戲劇或電影中演出。

■ The TV **drama** about spies was very suspenseful.
　那齣關於間諜的電視**劇**非常懸疑。

event 事件

發生的事情；特別的事。

■ The most exciting **event** in the story was the surprise ending.
　故事中最精彩的**事件**是意外的結局。

introduction 簡介

一篇簡短的文章，呈現並解釋小說或戲劇的劇情。

■ The **introduction** to *Frankenstein* is in the form of a letter.
《科學怪人》的**簡介**是以信件的型式呈現。

motive 動機

一股內在或外在的力量，迫使角色做出某些事情。

■ What was that character's **motive** for telling a lie?
那個角色說謊的**動機**為何？

passage 段落

書寫作品的部分內容，範圍短至一行，長至幾段。

■ His favorite **passage** from the book described the author's childhood.
他在書中最喜歡的**段落**描述了該作者的童年。

playwright 劇作家

戲劇的作者。

■ William Shakespeare is the world's most famous **playwright**.
威廉莎士比亞是世界上最知名的**劇作家**。

plot 情節

故事或戲劇中一連串的因果事件，導致最終結局。

■ The **plot** of that mystery story is filled with action.
該推理故事的**情節**充滿打鬥。

point of view 觀點

由角色的心理層面來看待故事發展的狀況。

■ The father's **point of view** about elopement was quite different from the daughter's. 父親對於私奔的**看法**與女兒迥然不同。

prologue 序幕

在戲劇第一幕開始前的介紹。

■ The playwright described the main characters in the **prologue** to the play.
劇作家在**序幕**中描述了主要角色。

quotation 名句

被引述的文句；某角色所說的詞語；在引號內的文字。

■ A popular **quotation** from *Julius Caesar* begins,"Friends, Romans, countrymen . . ."
《凱薩大帝》中**常被引用的文句**開頭是：「各位朋友，各位羅馬人，各位同胞……」。

role 角色

演員在劇中揣摩表演的人物。

■ Who would you like to see play the **role** of Romeo?
你想看誰飾演羅密歐這個**角色**呢？

sequence 順序

故事或事件發生的時序。

■ Sometimes actors rehearse their scenes out of **sequence**.
演員有時會不按**順序**排練他們出場的戲。

setting 情節背景

故事發生的地點與時間。

■ This play's **setting** is New York in the 1940s.
戲劇的**背景設定**於 1940 年代的紐約。

soliloquy 獨白

角色向觀眾發表想法的一番言論，猶如自言自語。

- One famous **soliloquy** is Hamlet's speech that begins, "To be, or not to be . . . "

  哈姆雷特中最知名的**獨白**是：「生，抑或是死⋯⋯」。

symbol 象徵

用以代表其他事物的人或物。

- In Hawthorne's famous novel, the scarlet letter is a **symbol** for adultery.

  在霍桑知名的小說中，紅字是姦淫罪的**象徵**。

theme 主題

戲劇或小說的主要意義；中心思想。

- Ambition and revenge are common **themes** in Shakespeare's plays.

  在莎士比亞的劇作中，雄心壯志與報復是常見的**主題**。

tragedy 悲劇

嚴肅且有悲傷結局的戲劇。

- *Macbeth*, the shortest of Shakespeare's plays, is a **tragedy**.

  莎士比亞最短的劇作《馬克白》是部悲劇。